A·HAUNTING
WE WILL GO

A-HAUNTING WE WILL GO

Ghostly Stories and Poems

selected by

Lee Bennett Hopkins

Albert Whitman & Company, Chicago

Copyright © 1977 by Lee Bennett Hopkins
Published simultaneously in Canada
by George J. McLeod, Limited, Toronto
Printed in the United States of America
All rights reserved
C.I.P. Information follows Acknowledgments

Acknowledgments

Every effort has been made to trace the ownership of all copyrighted material and to secure the necessary permissions to reprint these selections. In the event of any question arising as to the use of any material, the editor and the publisher, while expressing regret for any inadvertent error, will be happy to make the necessary correction in future printings. Thanks are due to the following for permission to reprint the copyrighted material listed below:

Wm. Collins + World Publishing Co. for "Here We Go" by Maria Leach, from THE THING AT THE FOOT OF THE BED AND OTHER SCARY TALES by Maria Leach. Copyright © 1959 by Maria Leach.

William Morrow & Co., Inc. for "The Dancing Jug" from THE WITCHES' RIDE AND OTHER TALES FROM COSTA RICA. Copyright © 1957 by Lupe de Osma.

Vanguard Press, Inc. for "The Stubbornest Man in Maine" reprinted from NEW ENGLAND BEAN-POT by M. Jagendorf by permission of the publisher, Vanguard Press, Inc. Copyright 1948 by M. A. Jagendorf. Copyright © renewed 1975 by M. Jagendorf.

Library of Congress Cataloging in Publication Data

Main entry under title:
A-haunting we will go.

CONTENTS: Ghosts pure and simple: Hillert, M. Nothing and nowhere. Ireland, E. How Horace learned to moan. Brooks, W. R. Jimmy takes vanishing lessons. Hopkins, L. B. The ninety-sixth ghost.—Is it or isn't it a ghost? Ghoulies and ghosties. Fisher, A. The ghost in the orchard. [etc.]
  1. Ghost stories, American. [1. Ghost stories. 2. Short stories] I. Hopkins, Lee Bennett. II. Rosenberry, Vera.

PZ5.H32   [Fic]   76-45449
ISBN 0-8075-3356-4

To Marijean Corrigan
who haunts me
with her charms!
LBH

CONTENTS

Part Two:

IS IT OR ISN'T IT A GHOST?

Part Three:

ONCE-UPON-A-TIME GHOSTS

INTRODUCTION

My Haunt and Other Haunts

When you think of ghosts, do you feel a little creepy and ready to look carefully over your shoulder? Do you expect formless shapes to float about in long white robes, clinking and clanking chains down stairways, sighing and scaring and calling "Boo-ooo!"?

Are ghosts really real? Do you believe in them?

For years and years, most of my life, I never believed in ghosts. I just shrugged and said something like, "Oh, come on now! How can anyone believe in ghosts?"

I had always lived in cities, and it just may be that cities are too crowded for ghosts who like their privacy when they go haunting. This meant that I never had any experience with ghosts and didn't believe in them until something happened to change my way of thinking.

13

I moved from the city to a magical, mysterious place along the Hudson River, to a house that sits atop a high riverbank. Down below I can see a cove from my balcony, a small, sheltered bay nestled in the shoreline of the Hudson. The cove was named for the original owner of the land, William Kemey, and to this day it is called Kemeys Cove.

What does this have to do with ghosts? I'll tell you. William Kemey came from a shipbuilding family. He sailed to America in 1790 and voyaged up the Hudson River, then called the North River. Falling in love with the beauty of the land, he decided to stay. He found a spot and built a low-ceilinged, English-style red brick house and called it Scarborough, after the town he'd come from in England.

Children, grandchildren, and great-grandchildren continued to live in the old Kemey house, until at last the property was sold. The first thing the new owner did was to tear down that fine old red brick house. Not a wall, not even a doorstep remained.

Over in the old Sparta cemetery, not far away, stand the tombstones of the Kemey family. People say that sometimes old William Kemey leaves his grave and returns to the spot by the cove where his fine house once stood. He comes there and calls to the boats sailing up and down the Hudson River. And strange though it seems, he knows even the newest boats by name. In his ghostly voice he calls to the boats and whether it be a warning or greeting, no one knows.

Have I ever heard that ghostly cry on a misty night? Yes, more than once. It happens especially when the moon is full and I step out on my balcony. I hear the ghostly English voice calling,

"Come over here, Sea Cat . . .
Come over here, Neptune's Night . . .
Come over here, Man o' the Whitecaps . . .
Over, over, over here!"

At this command, boats large and small make a sharp turn, pulling close to the river's edge, as near as it's safe to go. Their sails hang slack, their crews silently listen. Do they hear the voice, too? After a short time, the boats pull back and sail off for their own harbors.

Is my imagination playing tricks on me? Is it the ghost of old William Kemey calling or is it only a dog howling at the full moon? Could it be the breeze blowing through the old horse chestnut trees? Or the sound of a nearby brook? What *is* it I hear calling—

"Come over here, Sea Cat . . .
Come over here, Neptune's Night . . .
Come over here, Man o' the Whitecaps . . .
Over, over, over here!"

I don't know. As I said in the beginning, I never believed in ghosts. But William Kemey just may have changed my mind.

Yes, I'm commencing to think there are ghosts, or at least one—the ghost of old William Kemey. It started me reading and rereading stories about ghosts, all kinds of ghosts, good and bad. In

15

this book, there are tales and poems I want to share with you. Some are very old, some are brand new.

The stories are divided into three groups:

First comes "Ghosts Pure and Simple," with tales about ghosts who have problems of their own and sometimes problems made for them by living people. (Not everyone is afraid of ghosts!)

Next, in "Is It or Isn't It a Ghost?" there are stories about girls and boys puzzled by ghostly encounters. You'll have to decide for yourself how you'd feel in adventures like these.

And last, "Once-Upon-a-Time Ghosts" features old tales about ghosts and spirits and strange little ghosties who come haunting when someone begins, "Once upon a time. . . ." These are stories told in England, Scotland, America, India, and Costa Rica, proving that ghosts have no one homeland.

Some of the tales will surprise you and make you laugh. Others just might send a cheerful shudder or shiver through your bones. All of them might set you wondering about ghosts as much as I do.

And now, if you'll sit right down and begin to read, a-haunting we will go!

LEE BENNETT HOPKINS
Scarborough, New York

GHOSTS
pure and simple

NOTHING
AND NOWHERE

If it can't be seen
And it can't be heard,
If there's a whisper
And never a word,
If it isn't in here
And it's not out there,
Then it's time to be careful,
Time to beware.

If it can't be touched
And it can't be felt,
If it can't be tasted
And it can't be smelt,
If it just isn't anything,
Then it's the most
Of whatever it takes
To be a—GHOST!

Margaret Hillert

Elizabeth Ireland

HOW HORACE LEARNED TO MOAN

Horace was a happy ghost. He lived with his father and mother in a big old house with lots of creaking stairs and windows that rattled. It was just right for ghosts.

Of course, people lived there too—a whole family of people—but they all got along very well together. The ghosts didn't mind the noise the people made daytimes, and the people didn't mind the noise the ghosts made at night.

There was only one trouble.

Horace!

Horace was a well-behaved little ghost in some ways. He had learned his vanishing lessons perfectly. One moment he was there

20

and then—whisk!—he wasn't. Sometimes he vanished for his family's visitors at after-midnight tea, and they all said they had never seen finer vanishing. Besides, he could creak doors, and he rattled windows as well as a grown-up ghost.

But he couldn't moan, and he couldn't groan, and when he tried to clank his chain, it jingled!

"What is wrong, Horace?" his father and mother asked him often. "It's perfectly silly for a bright little ghost like you not to moan and groan. What is that horrible noise you make?"

"People call it laughing," Horace said. "I'm sorry. I just can't moan and groan. I'm too happy! I haven't anything to moan and groan about!"

His father and mother would groan softly, and float upstairs to talk things over.

Horace wandered around, creaking a stair or two and rattling at the second-biggest window just for practice.

Once he laughed. When he did, the people upstairs woke up suddenly and sat up in their beds and said, "What was that?"

"Oh, dear!" Horace said to himself. And he put one hand over his mouth and kept it there till daylight to make sure he wouldn't laugh again.

"Horace," his mother said when he went upstairs to go to bed that morning, "today you must stay up at least till noon. Maybe that will teach you to moan and groan."

"All right, Mother," Horace said cheerfully. He felt a little queer inside, though. He had never been up after sunrise in his whole life.

He floated downstairs very slowly and started to haunt the breakfast room. He felt ever so jiggly as he peeped inside for the first time. How bright it was!

And it was positively full of people laughing and talking and drinking milk and orange juice and eating breakfast food.

Horace took a deep breath, stepped out beside the kitchen cabinet, and vanished.

The littlest boy at the breakfast table saw him. He gurgled and waved his spoon. Horace vanished again beside the refrigerator.

"Funny thing," the father said, and rubbed his eyes. "I could swear the refrigerator door was open just a minute ago. But it isn't."

Horace vanished again behind a window curtain.

"Mother, there's a ghost behind the curtain," the next-to-littlest boy said.

"Finish your cereal, Tommy, and stop trying to fool me," the mother laughed.

And after that nobody paid any attention to Horace! Even when he laughed, somebody else laughed too, and nobody noticed him. Finally he perched on top of the refrigerator and watched the family finish breakfast.

Then he went outside. It was queer and scary in the bright sunlight with no nice comfortable dark, no big hoot owls and

22

whippoorwills singing songs that Horace loved, and no dogs howling far over the hills. But pretty soon he found out he was getting used to the daytime and the songs of the other birds and all the queer daytime sounds. There wasn't a single thing scary about them, once you knew what made them.

He wandered around having a fine time, though he did get a bit sleepy. As the big grandfather clock struck noon, he whisked upstairs and woke up his mother.

She looked at him anxiously. "Did you learn to moan and groan, Horace?"

Horace shook his head. "No. I found out that daylight is just as nice and friendly as dark!"

"Oh, dear!" his mother groaned. "Well, go to bed, Horace. But whatever you do, don't laugh! Mother needs her sleep. I've tossed and turned all day."

Horace went to his own room, yawning. He didn't laugh but he couldn't keep from chuckling a little bit.

That night his mother and father had a ghost visitor to after-midnight tea.

When she heard Horace laugh, she shrieked, "Dear me! What a horrible child! Really, he takes the curl right out of my hair. Why don't you do something about that laughing?"

"What can we do?" Horace's mother moaned.

"Shut him in a lighted room with lots of people," the visiting ghost snapped. "If that does not teach him to moan and groan, I don't know what will!"

"It sounds cruel," Horace's father said, "but I think we had better try it."

A week later, sure enough, Horace's mother marched him downstairs and opened the big living room door a tiny crack.

"There!! Inside with you! And mind you stay at least an hour!"

Horace didn't come back upstairs for three whole hours!

His mother was walking up and down, wringing her hands, when he appeared.

"Oh, darling, I shouldn't have done it! Forgive me, Horace! Was it so terrible?"

"I had a wonderful time, Mother!" Horace said. "It was a Halloween Party. Everybody was dressed up. There were three other ghosts like me, only I think they were really people. We played games. I won a prize, too. A horn!"

"Ooooh!" his father groaned. "Where is it? Did you learn to play it?"

Horace shook his head. "No. I gave it to another little ghost who couldn't vanish the way I did when we played hide-and-seek."

Horace's father and mother looked at each other and sighed.

"All right, Horace, go rattle your chain for a while," his mother said, "and remember, *do* try not to jingle."

"Yes, Mother," Horace said happily and floated off.

How Horace Learned to Moan

"At least he didn't bring the horn home," his father said. "That's one thing to be thankful for."

Loud jingling sounded from the next room. Horace's father and mother groaned, clapped their hands over their ears and vanished.

But the very next evening something happened. Horace and his family woke up just at sundown and smelled something perfectly delicious!

"What is that *wonderful* smell?" Horace asked.

His mother and father exchanged a mysterious smile.

"It's ghosts' favorite food—and that's all I will tell you now," his father said.

And his mother said, "Hurry and put on a clean sheet. It looks as if we're going to have a party tonight!"

They floated downstairs in a great hurry, and out the hall to the kitchen. They stopped by the door.

In the kitchen Tommy was saying to his mother, "But what happens to the middle of the doughnuts, Mother?"

His mother laughed. "Why, doughnut middles are the favorite food of ghosts, Tommy! See that big bowl that looks empty? It's full to the top with doughnut middles!"

Horace jiggled up and down excitedly. He had often heard about doughnut middles, but he'd never eaten one. He could hardly wait to try them!

As soon as the people had taken their doughnuts to the dining room, the ghosts swished into the kitchen and began eating doughnut middles.

Horace's mother ate only two dozen, because she was on a diet.

Horace's father ate four dozen.

And Horace finished the whole bowlful! Ummm, were they good!

But a little while later, when his mother and father looked for Horace, they couldn't find him anywhere. He wasn't in the cellar or the attic or the garden or downstairs.

At last they found him curled up in bed in his own room.

"Ooooh," he said, "I have a pain!"

"Horace!" his parents beamed. "You *groaned!*"

"OOOOoooooOOOOO!" said Horace. "It *hurts!*"

"Horace!" His parents both hugged him. "You moaned, too!"

"Yes," Horace said, "because I have a pain in my middle. How about some spirits of peppermint or something? OOOh. OOOOoooOOO!"

And ever since, Horace has been able to moan and groan beautifully. Even if he's happy, all he has to do is think about the time he ate too many doughnut middles. It always works.

But he still can't clank his chain!

Walter R. Brooks

JIMMY TAKES VANISHING LESSONS

The school bus picked up Jimmy Crandall every morning at the side road that led up to his aunt's house, and every afternoon it dropped him there again. And so twice a day, on the bus, he passed the entrance to the mysterious road.

It wasn't much of a road any more. It was choked with weeds and blackberry bushes, and the woods on both sides pressed in so closely that the branches met overhead, and it was dark and gloomy even on bright days. The bus driver once pointed it out.

"Folks that go in there after dark," he said, "well, they usually don't ever come out again. There's a haunted house about a quarter of a mile down that road." He paused. "But you ought to know about that, Jimmy. It was your grandfather's house."

28

Jimmy knew about it, and he knew that it now belonged to his Aunt Mary. But Jimmy's aunt would never talk to him about the house. She said the stories about it were silly nonsense and there were no such things as ghosts. If all the villagers weren't a lot of superstitious idiots, she would be able to rent the house, and then she would have enough money to buy Jimmy some decent clothes and take him to the movies.

Jimmy thought it was all very well to say that there were no such things as ghosts, but how about the people who had tried to live there? Aunt Mary had rented the house three times, but every family had moved out within a week. They said the things that went on there were just too queer. So nobody would live in it any more.

Jimmy thought about the house a lot. If he could only prove that there wasn't a ghost. . . . And one Saturday when his aunt was in the village, Jimmy took the key to the haunted house from its hook on the kitchen door, and started out.

It had seemed like a fine idea when he had first thought of it—to find out for himself. Even in the silence and damp gloom of the old road it still seemed pretty good. Nothing to be scared of, he told himself. Ghosts aren't around in the daytime. But when he came out in the clearing and looked at those blank, dusty windows, he wasn't so sure.

"Oh, come on!" he told himself. And he squared his shoulders and waded through the long grass to the porch.

29

Then he stopped again. His feet did not seem to want to go up the steps. It took him nearly five minutes to persuade them to move. But when at last they did, they marched right up and across the porch to the front door, and Jimmy set his teeth hard and put the key in the keyhole. It turned with a squeak. He pushed the door open and went in.

That was probably the bravest thing that Jimmy had ever done. He was in a long dark hall with closed doors on both sides, and on the right the stairs went up. He had left the door open behind him, and the light from it showed him that, except for the hatrack and table and chairs, the hall was empty. And then as he stood there, listening to the bumping of his heart, gradually the light faded, the hall grew darker and darker—as if something huge had come up on the porch behind him and stood there, blocking the doorway. He swung round quickly, but there was nothing there.

He drew a deep breath. It must have been just a cloud passing across the sun. But then the door, all of itself, began to swing shut. And before he could stop it, it closed with a bang. And it was then, as he was pulling frantically at the handle to get out, that Jimmy saw the ghost.

It behaved just as you would expect a ghost to behave. It was a tall, dim, white figure, and it came gliding slowly down the stairs towards him. Jimmy gave a yell, yanked the door open, and tore down the steps.

30

He didn't stop until he was well down the road. Then he had to get his breath. He sat down on a log. "Boy!" he said. "I've seen a ghost! Golly, was that awful!" Then after a minute, he thought, "What was so awful about it? He was trying to scare me, like that smart aleck who was always jumping out from behind things. Pretty silly business for a grown-up ghost to be doing."

It always makes you mad when someone deliberately tries to scare you. And as Jimmy got over his fright, he began to get angry. And pretty soon he got up and started back. "I must get that key, anyway," he thought, for he had left it in the door.

This time he approached very quietly. He thought he'd just lock the door and go home. But as he tiptoed up the steps he saw it was still open; and as he reached out cautiously for the key, he heard a faint sound. He drew back and peeked around the door jamb, and there was the ghost.

The ghost was going back upstairs, but he wasn't gliding now, he was doing a sort of dance, and every other step he would bend double and shake with laughter. His thin cackle was the sound Jimmy had heard. Evidently he was enjoying the joke he had played. That made Jimmy madder than ever. He stuck his head farther around the door jamb and yelled "Boo!" at the top of his lungs. The ghost gave a thin shriek and leaped two feet in the air, then collapsed on the stairs.

As soon as Jimmy saw he could scare the ghost even worse than

31

the ghost could scare him, he wasn't afraid any more, and he came right into the hall. The ghost was hanging on to the bannisters and panting. "Oh, my goodness!" he gasped. "Oh, my gracious! You can't *do* that to me!"

"I did it, didn't I?" said Jimmy. "Now we're even."

"Nothing of the kind," said the ghost crossly. "You seem pretty stupid, even for a boy. Ghosts are supposed to scare people. People aren't supposed to scare ghosts." He got up slowly and glided down and sat on the bottom step. "But look here, boy; this could be pretty serious for me if people got to know about it."

"You mean you don't want me to tell anybody about it?" Jimmy asked.

"Suppose we make a deal," the ghost said. "You keep still about this, and in return I'll—well, let's see; how would you like to know how to vanish?"

"Oh, that would be swell!" Jimmy exclaimed. "But—can you vanish?"

"Sure," said the ghost, and he did. All at once he just wasn't there. Jimmy was alone in the hall.

But his voice went right on. "It would be pretty handy, wouldn't it?" he said persuasively. "You could get into the movies free whenever you wanted to, and if your aunt called you to do something—when you were in the yard, say—well, she wouldn't be able to find you."

32

"I don't mind helping Aunt Mary," Jimmy said.

"H'm. High-minded, eh?" said the ghost. "Well, then—"

"I wish you'd please reappear," Jimmy interrupted. "It makes me feel funny to talk to somebody who isn't there."

"Sorry, I forgot," said the ghost, and there he was again, sitting on the bottom step. Jimmy could see the step, dimly, right through him. "Good trick, eh? Well, if you don't like vanishing, maybe I could teach you to seep through keyholes. Like this." He floated over to the door and went right through the keyhole, the way water goes down the drain. Then he came back the same way.

"That's useful, too," he said. "Getting into locked rooms and so on. You can go anywhere the wind can."

"No," said Jimmy. "There's only one thing you can do to get me to promise not to tell about scaring you. Go live somewhere else. There's Miller's, up the road. Nobody lives there any more."

"That old shack!" said the ghost, with a nasty laugh. "Doors and windows half off, roof leaky—no thanks! What do you think it's like in a storm, windows banging, rain dripping on you—I guess not! Peace and quiet, that's really what a ghost wants out of life."

"Well, I don't think it's very fair," Jimmy said, "for you to live in a house that doesn't belong to you and keep my aunt from renting it."

"Pooh!" said the ghost. "I'm not stopping her from renting it. I don't take up any room, and it's not my fault if people get scared and leave."

33

"It certainly is!" Jimmy said angrily. "You don't play fair, and I'm not going to make any bargain with you. I'm going to tell everybody how I scared you."

"Oh, you mustn't do that!" The ghost seemed quite disturbed and he vanished and reappeared rapidly several times. "If that got out, every ghost in the country would be in terrible trouble."

So they argued about it. The ghost said if Jimmy wanted money he could learn to vanish; then he could join a circus and get a big salary. Jimmy said he didn't want to be in a circus; he wanted to go to college and learn to be a doctor. He was very firm. And the ghost began to cry. "But this is my *home*," he said. "Thirty years I've lived here and no trouble to anybody, and now you want to throw me out into the cold world! And for what? A little money! That's pretty heartless." And he sobbed, trying to make Jimmy feel cruel.

Jimmy didn't feel cruel at all, for the ghost had certainly driven plenty of other people out into the cold world. But he didn't really think it would do much good for him to tell anybody that he had scared the ghost. Nobody would believe him, and how could he prove it? So after a minute he said, "Well, all right. You teach me to vanish and I won't tell." They settled it that way.

Jimmy didn't say anything to his aunt about what he'd done. But every Saturday he went to the haunted house for his vanishing lesson. It is really quite easy when you know how, and in a couple of weeks he could flicker, and in six weeks the ghost gave him an examination and he got a B-plus, which is very good for a human. So he thanked the ghost and shook hands with him and said, "Well, good-by now. You'll hear from me."

"What do you mean by that?" said the ghost suspiciously. But Jimmy just laughed and ran off home.

That night at supper Jimmy's aunt said, "Well, what have you been doing today?"

"I've been learning to vanish."

His aunt smiled and said, "That must be fun."

"Honestly," said Jimmy. "The ghost up at grandfather's taught me."

"I don't think that's very funny," said his aunt. "And will you please not—why, where are you?" she demanded, for he had vanished.

"Here, Aunt Mary," he said as he reappeared.

"Merciful heavens!" she exclaimed, and she pushed back her chair and rubbed her eyes hard. Then she looked at him again.

Well, it took a lot of explaining and he had to do it twice more before he could persuade her that he really could vanish. She was pretty upset. But at last she calmed down and they had a long talk. Jimmy kept his word and didn't tell her that he had scared the ghost, but he said he had a plan, and at last, though very reluctantly, she agreed to help him.

So the next day she went up to the old house and started to work.

35

She opened the windows and swept and dusted and aired the bedding, and made as much noise as possible. This disturbed the ghost, and pretty soon he came floating into the room where she was sweeping. She was scared all right. She gave a yell and threw the broom at him. As the broom went right through him and he came nearer, waving his arms and groaning, she shrank back.

And Jimmy, who had been standing there invisible all the time, suddenly appeared and jumped at the ghost with a "Boo!" and the ghost fell over in a dead faint.

As soon as Jimmy's aunt saw that, she wasn't frightened any more. She found some smelling salts and held them under the ghost's nose, and when he came to she tried to help him into a chair. Of course she couldn't help him much because her hands went right through him. But at last he sat up and said reproachfully to Jimmy, "You broke your word!"

"I promised not to tell about scaring you," said the boy, "but I didn't promise not to scare you again."

And his aunt said, "You really are a ghost, aren't you? I thought you were just stories people made up. Well, excuse me, but I must get on with my work." And she began sweeping and banging around with her broom harder than ever.

The ghost put his hands to his head. "All this noise," he said. "Couldn't you work more quietly, ma'am?"

"Whose house is this, anyway?" she demanded. "If you don't like it, why don't you move out?"

The ghost sneezed violently several times. "Excuse me," he said. "You're raising so much dust. Where's that boy?" he asked suddenly. For Jimmy had vanished again.

"I'm sure I don't know," she replied. "Probably getting ready to scare you again."

"You ought to have better control of him," said the ghost severely. "If he was my boy, I'd take a hairbrush to him."

"You have my permission," she said, and she reached right through the ghost and pulled the chair cushion out from under him and began banging the dust out of it. "What's more," she went on, as he got up and glided wearily to another chair, "Jimmy and I are going to sleep here nights from now on, and I don't think it would be very smart of you to try any tricks."

"Ha, ha," said the ghost nastily. "He who laughs last—"

"Ha, ha, yourself," said Jimmy's voice from close behind him. "And that's me, laughing last."

The ghost muttered and vanished.

Jimmy's aunt put cotton in her ears and slept that night in the best bedroom with the light lit. The ghost screamed for a while down in the cellar, but nothing happened, so he came upstairs. He thought he would appear to her as two glaring, fiery eyes, which was one of his best tricks, but first he wanted to be sure where Jimmy was. But he couldn't find him. He hunted all over the house, and though he was invisible himself, he got more and more nervous. He kept imagining that at any moment Jimmy might jump out at him from some dark corner and scare him into fits. Finally he got so jittery that he went back to the cellar and hid in the coal bin all night.

The following days were just as bad for the ghost. Several times he tried to scare Jimmy's aunt while she was working, but she didn't scare worth a cent, and twice Jimmy managed to sneak up on him and appear suddenly with a loud yell, frightening him dreadfully. He was, I suppose, rather timid even for a ghost. He began to look quite haggard. He had several long arguments with Jimmy's aunt, in which he wept and appealed to her sympathy, but she was firm. If he wanted to live there he would have to pay rent, just like anybody else. There was the abandoned Miller farm two miles up the road. Why didn't he move there?

When the house was all in apple-pie order, Jimmy's aunt went down to the village to see a Mr. and Mrs. Whistler, who were living at the hotel because they couldn't find a house to move into. She told them about the old house, but they said, "No, thank you. We've heard about that house. It's haunted. I'll bet," they said, "*you* wouldn't dare spend a night there."

She told them that she had spent the last week there, but they evidently didn't believe her. So she said, "You know my nephew, Jimmy. He's twelve years old. I am so sure that the house is not haunted that, if you want to rent it, I will let Jimmy stay there with

38

you every night until you are sure everything is all right."

"Ha!" said Mr. Whistler. "The boy won't do it. He's got more sense."

So they sent for Jimmy. "Why, I've spent the last week there," he said. "Sure. I'd just as soon."

But the Whistlers still refused.

So Jimmy's aunt went around and told a lot of the village people about their talk, and everybody made so much fun of the Whistlers for being afraid, when a twelve-year-old boy wasn't, that they were ashamed, and said they would rent it. So they moved in. Jimmy stayed there for a week, but he saw nothing of the ghost. And then one day one of the boys in his grade told him that somebody had seen a ghost up at the Miller farm. So Jimmy knew the ghost had taken his aunt's advice.

A day or two later he walked up to the Miller farm. There was no front door, and he walked right in. There was some groaning and thumping upstairs, and then after a minute the ghost came floating down.

"Oh, it's you!" he said. "Goodness sakes, can't you leave me in peace?"

Jimmy said he'd just come up to see how he was getting along.

"Getting along fine," said the ghost. "From my point of view it's a very desirable property. Peaceful. Quiet. Nobody playing silly tricks."

39

"Well," said Jimmy, "I won't bother you if you don't bother the Whistlers. But if you come back there—"

"Don't worry," said the ghost.

So with the rent money, Jimmy and his aunt had a much easier life. They went to the movies sometimes twice a week, and Jimmy had all new clothes, and on Thanksgiving, for the first time in his life, Jimmy had a turkey. Once a week he would go up to the Miller farm to see the ghost and they got to be very good friends. The ghost even came down to the Thanksgiving dinner, though of course he couldn't eat much. He seemed to enjoy the warmth of the house, and he was in very good humor. He taught Jimmy several more tricks. The best one was how to glare with fiery eyes, which was useful later on when Jimmy became a doctor and had to look down people's throats to see if their tonsils ought to come out. He was really a pretty good fellow as ghosts go, and Jimmy's aunt got quite fond of him herself. When the real winter weather began, she even used to worry about him a lot, because of course there was no heat in the Miller place and the doors and windows didn't amount to much and there was hardly any roof. The ghost tried to explain to her that heat and cold didn't bother ghosts at all.

"Maybe not," she said, "but just the same, it can't be very pleasant." And when he accepted their invitation for Christmas dinner she knitted some red woolen slippers, and he was so pleased that he broke down and cried. And that made Jimmy's aunt so

40

happy, *she* broke down and cried.

Jimmy didn't cry, but he said, "Aunt Mary, don't you think it would be nice if the ghost came down and lived with us this winter?"

"I would feel very much better about him if he did," she said.

So he stayed with them that winter, and then he just stayed on, and it must have been a peaceful place for the last I heard he was still there.

Lee Bennett Hopkins

THE NINETY-SIXTH GHOST

Agnes Anna Elkins lived in one of the most expensive and lavish mansions in all of Spartatown. People from miles and miles and miles away would come for Sunday drives just to pass by and look at her magnificent place. It seemed that everyone knew of Agnes Anna Elkins's house, but few could understand how she, a poor old woman, could afford such a place on so much fine land. What people did not know was that Agnes Anna Elkins had one very extraordinary talent. She was the cleverest woman in the whole of Spartatown when it came to dealing with ghosts, and that was the key to her ownership of the place.

42

When Peter John Knight, the original owner of the mansion, bought the house it was filled with ghosts. Ghosts banged in the attic, they made eerie clanging sounds all night long in the closed-off rooms upstairs—so eerie that Peter John Knight never went into them or opened them up.

Ghosts filled the hallways, the stairwells, and haunted all the closets in the house, including the kitchen pantry. Knowing the reputation of Agnes Anna Elkins, Peter John Knight called her in one morning to discuss his ghostly problems.

"Why, you've no problems at all," Agnes Anna Elkins told him. "Leave me alone in this house for one whole night when the moon is at its fullest and brightest. I will rid your entire house of all your pesty ghosts."

On the night of April 13, when the moon was at its fullest and brightest of any day that year, Agnes Anna Elkins walked up the great path leading to the house of Peter John Knight.

"Leave me here until dawn—alone," she said. "When you return tomorrow morning, your ghosts will have disappeared from the house. All of them."

And in one night she did just that!

The next morning, about an hour after dawn, Peter John Knight returned to his house and found that Agnes Anna Elkins had already left.

On the kitchen table there was a note that read:

43

Dear Peter John Knight:

As I promised you, the ghosts are all gone. You won't be bothered with them anymore. I cleaned them all out for you. No wonder you were troubled with them. I counted ninety-five in all. Ninety-five!

Since it didn't take me any longer than an hour or so (you know how good I am at collecting ghosts), I had the time to clean up the closed-off rooms upstairs. My word, were they ever dirty!

You shouldn't ever be bothered again with ghosts in your house. But if you are, please call on me again.

Yours truly,
Agnes Anna Elkins

Peter John Knight lived happily ever after without the ghosts ever bothering him or haunting him again. His house was livable again, unhaunted, and he was so peaceful in the beautiful old mansion because of the work of Agnes Anna Elkins that he decided to leave her the house when he passed on. And he did.

That was how Agnes Anna Elkins, a poor old woman, came to own the house and all the fine land it stood upon.

But lo and alas! On the very first night that Agnes Anna Elkins moved into the house, she knew there was something wrong. She was positive there was a ghost lurking somewhere in the house, so she set out to look for it. She looked everywhere—in every room, in the hallways, on the stairwells, in all of the closets. But there wasn't a ghost to be found anywhere.

44

"I must be getting old," said Agnes Anna Elkins to herself because there was no one else in the house to talk to. "I may be imagining a ghost."

The house was chilled with November air so Agnes Anna Elkins decided to brew herself a cup of tea, sit by the fireplace, and rock a good part of the night away. When she went into the kitchen pantry for some tea she noticed, on the very top shelf, an old copper kettle.

"How nice this is," she thought. "There's nothing as nice as an old copper kettle to boil water in."

She filled the copper kettle with water and put it on the stove to boil. When the steam shot out from the kettle's spout, Agnes Anna Elkins turned off the stove and poured the boiling water into a cup to brew her tea.

Behind her she heard a slight noise. Turning around, she saw a ghost standing on top of a kitchen chair and looking down at her.

"Well, how d'ya do do do-ooOOOOooo, Agnes Anna Elkins," said the ghost.

"Fine, thank you," answered Agnes Anna Elkins calmly. "Fine indeed. But do tell me something. How do you know my name, pray tell?"

"Oh, your name is known to me very, very well," the ghost answered. "I remember how you cleaned out all my fellow-ghosts from this house when Peter John Knight owned it. All ninety-five of

45

them. But you weren't clever enough to track me down and catch me the way you did all the others."

"Oh? And where did you come from?" Agnes Anna Elkins asked. "Where have you been hiding?"

"I haven't been hiding," replied the ghost. "I came from the bottom of that copper kettle, where I've been for at least fifty years now—long before you or Peter John Knight lived here. You see, I can only appear from the copper kettle when the water boils. The steam allows me to appear. There haven't been any tea drinkers around this place, so I've been forced to stay at the bottom of the copper kettle."

"Now listen here, ghost," Agnes Anna Elkins said. "Do you really think that I would believe that a big ghost the likes of you could appear out of that teeny, tiny hole in the kettle's spout? I don't believe you at all!"

"Well I did," said the ghost. "Besides, who are YOU not to believe ME? You'd better be careful, old woman, or I'll haunt this entire house—upstairs and down—all by my ghostly self. I'll make you wish that you never came to live here! I'll scare you so badly that your hair will stand up from fear, like uncooked spaghetti, your knees will shake like you're dancing a jig, and your heart will quiver like liver. I'll scare you so much that you'll walk around this house like a bowl of Jell-o. That's what I'll do to you."

"Now, now, now!" said Agnes Anna Elkins becoming annoyed at

46

the ghost. "That's no way for a ghost to talk. I'm not afraid of you or your haunting threats. Don't you think you're being unkind to talk to me this way?"

"I'm sorry," said the ghost, "but just a little bit sorry. I don't like people who doubt my words."

"Well it just seems impossible to me that you could come out of that teeny, tiny hole in the kettle's spout, that's all. I'm just positive you didn't. I'm more positive that such a thing cannot be done—even by the cleverest of ghosts."

Agnes Anna Elkins thought for a second or two.

"If you can come through that teeny, tiny hole in the kettle's

spout, I'll bet you can easily go in and out of this empty jelly jar," she said, taking a jelly jar down from the pantry shelf. "But I think you're fooling me. I don't believe you came through the teeny, tiny hole in the kettle spout, and I don't believe you could even go through the hole in the top of this jelly jar which is much, much bigger than the teeny, tiny hole in the kettle spout. I think you are a fake."

At that, the ghost became very, very angry and he repeated all his threats.

"You've made me very, very angry, Agnes Anna Elkins! I'm going to scare you so badly that your hair will stand up from fear like uncooked spaghetti, your knees will shake like you're dancing a jig, and your heart will quiver like liver. I'm going to scare you so much that you'll walk around this house like a bowl of Jell-o, that's what I'm going to do. I don't know how you tricked the other ninety-five ghosts into leaving this house, but you're not wise enough to trick me. You're just a silly old woman, Agnes Anna Elkins. But before I begin to scare you and truly haunt you out of your wits, I'm going to prove to you that I can get through the hole in your jelly jar—and right out again."

"Never, ever," teased Agnes Anna Elkins. "You won't be able to do it. Never!"

"Watch this," said the ghost. "Here I go."

Within a half a second, the ghost disappeared into the opening of

48

the jelly jar. Faster than that, Agnes Anna Elkins tightly screwed the top on the jelly jar closed. She turned it so tightly that the ghost couldn't possibly escape. Never!

Agnes Anna Elkins then took the tightly closed jelly jar outside to the stream that ran from a mountaintop into a wide and deep river. She kneeled down and placed the jar in the stream and watched it float off into the river.

The ninety-sixth ghost was gone, gone, *gone*.

"Humph!" said Agnes Anna Elkins. "It is such a shame to have to lose that jelly jar. Jelly jars aren't easy to come by anymore. But it's better to lose a jelly jar than to have to put up with a nasty ghost the like of that one. He was by far the nastiest ghost I ever did see!"

Like Peter John Knight, Agnes Anna Elkins lived happily ever after in her mansion. And never, ever was she bothered again by a ghost. Never, ever.

Is it or isn't it
a GHOST?

GHOULIES AND GHOSTIES:
AN OLD SPELL

From ghoulies and ghosties,
Long-leggity beasties,
And things that go *bump* in the night,
Good Lord deliver us.

Aileen Fisher

THE GHOST IN THE ORCHARD

Freddy tiptoed across the creaky kitchen floor and looked out the window. The stars were bright. Above the hills hung a piece of moon like a round white cracker with a big bite taken out. The potato patch seemed almost light behind the row of currant bushes now bare of leaves.

Freddy could see as far as the orchard. But there the shadows began—right where the ghost liked to move about among the apple trees!

Many of the apple trees still had their leaves, browned by late October frosts, clinging stubbornly to the branches. And some of the trees still had late apples. But the ghost did not seem to like to

54

climb up into the high branches where the best apples hung. It stayed on the ground, white and graceful, drifting in and out among the trees. At least, that is what it did the two times Freddy had seen it, once last week and again two nights ago.

Freddy hadn't breathed a word about his ghost to anyone. Pop would be sure to say it was only a dream. Mom would say it was that extra piece of cake—she *knew* Freddy shouldn't eat another piece of cake! And his two little sisters, well, they were too young to know about ghosts anyway. Besides, Freddy had to get one really good look before he was sure himself.

The wind blew a thin white scarf of cloud over the moon. That made the potato patch darker and the orchard even more shadowy than before. Then the bony fingers of a poplar branch began to scratch against the window sill. Scratch, scratch!

Freddy stood still as stone at the window and watched. He was not sure if he wanted the ghost to come. With Mom and Pop at the Grange meeting, and the two little girls sound asleep upstairs, he was all alone. But as long as the ghost stayed out in the orchard and he was safe in the house, it would be all right.

Tick, tick, tick! went the clock on top of the stove, as loud as if it were ticking through a loudspeaker. Freddy creaked across the floor to see what time it was. Almost nine. Mom told him they wanted to find him in bed when they got home around 9:30. Well, the ghost had better hurry.

Freddy went to the window again. Pop had left the garage doors open in the middle of the barn, so the building looked like a big face with its mouth open—a mouth full of darkness.

Just then something like the swish of a ghost brushed against Freddy's leg. He jumped! His throat seemed to close up, pinching off his voice.

Then it came again, that brush against his leg. Freddy held his breath and heard his heart thumping up and down in his ears.

For the third time his leg was touched. But now there was a familiar purring sound with it that set Freddy's heart to beating in the right place once more. He gave a big sigh of relief and stooped down.

"Mouser," he said, "you scared me out of a year's growth. I thought you were a ghost! How did you get in here? You're supposed to be out in the barn catching mice." Mouser arched her back and purred and rubbed herself some more.

At the window again, Freddy felt much more brave, with Mouser around. Not that Mouser had ever caught a ghost! But just to know she was close and awake, that was something. Wait! What was that? What was that white thing out in the orchard, gliding behind the trunks of the trees? It must be the ghost! What else could it be? Freddy pressed his forehead against the cold glass and strained his eyes, trying to get a good look.

The moon was sailing free of clouds again for a minute. But the

56

ghost had a teasing way of staying in the shadows, back in the orchard, instead of moving out into the open. For a fleeting second Freddy caught the glint of moonlight on its head. Was it really a head, or a hat with some strange decorations? He had never heard of a ghost wearing a hat, still . . .

There was a sudden noise at the front of the house. Freddy drew back from the window and listened. Someone, or something, was at the front door. What was this anyway, with a ghost in the orchard, and a knock at the front door?

Freddy tiptoed toward the living room, where the lights were still lit. Quickly he ducked into the bedroom which opened off to one side. From there he could see the front door, see who was knocking. He peeked out.

Knock, knock! Well, it wasn't a ghost, at least. Instead of being flimsy and white, it was big and black and wore a wide-brimmed hat. That hat! Freddy knew it at once. It belonged to Big Pete who lived in a log cabin back toward the hills, Big Pete who helped Pop whenever there was extra work on the farm.

Freddy hurried to the front door and opened it. "Hello," he said. "Sorry I didn't get here sooner. I was out in the kitchen."

"Your pa home, is he? Coming up from town I saw your lights still on and figured I'd find out where your pa wanted the poles put I cut over on Red Hill . . ." Big Pete talked in a tone of voice that never went up and never went down, but just stayed straight and flat like a

57

pavement running on and on. And his sentences never had any commas or periods.

"Mom and Pop went to the Grange meeting. But they won't be late." Freddy stopped. Part of him wanted Big Pete to stay and talk, and another part wanted him to go. If Big Pete stayed, Freddy wouldn't be all alone with the ghost. On the other hand, he wouldn't be able to get a good look at it, with company around. "Ah . . . won't you come in and wait?" he finished.

"Guess I'll be moving along. It's pretty late for me to be up and about of a night and I can stop by and see your pa in the morning about the poles." Big Pete turned to go. "Cut a nice lot of spruce poles for him on the north slope of Red Hill . . . nothing like a north slope to make good spruce poles."

"Wait a minute." Freddy wasn't sure just what he wanted to say to Big Pete. Still, he didn't want him to go quite yet. "Do you . . . do you believe in ghosts?"

Big Pete turned back and looked at Freddy, who tried to keep from shivering as he stood in the open doorway with the night air upon him. "You ain't seen any around here have you? Can't say as I either believe in them or don't believe in them but my grandmother now . . . she was a great one for believing in ghosts, she was."

"Won't you come in a minute? It's cold, and I'd like to know about your grandmother."

"Reckon I can stay a minute or two if you're a mind to hear about

58

ghosts," Big Pete drawled. He kept right on talking, with his voice in a straight line, as he came in the door and stood there while Freddy quickly closed it. "My grandmother, she was on real friendly terms with ghosts she was . . . always talking to them and seeing them sitting around the house."

"Around the house!"

"Yep, and especially the ghost of her mother sitting in her special rocking chair in the front room just like she used to sit when my grandmother was a girl."

Freddy looked out of the corner of his eye at the nearby chairs. "Did your grandmother's ghost ever wear a hat?"

"Not that I ever heard tell of. My grandmother used to see her mother plain as day sitting there though no one else in the family ever could. Something about my grandmother made her see things other folks couldn't."

"I'd rather have the ghosts stay outside somewhere . . . like in the orchard. Did your grandmother ever see any in your orchard?"

"Not that I recall she didn't. I never heard of any ghosts sticking around any orchards." Big Pete kept turning his hat around and around in his hands, as if talking about ghosts made him a little nervous. "Well, I reckon you better stop thinking about ghosts, or you won't get any sleep tonight and me neither." He put his hand on the doorknob. "You ain't scared to stay here till your folks get home are you?"

"Me? No. Why, I take care of the place lots of times." Freddy tried to sound brave, but he didn't feel so brave inside.

"You can tell your pa I'll be down to see him about the poles in the morning . . . nice straight poles off the north side of Red Hill." Still talking, he went out into the night and closed the door behind him.

Freddy took a deep breath. He gave a sideways glance at the old rocker with its padded seat, and was glad to see that it was empty. Would the ghost still be waiting out in the orchard, he wondered? Or would it be frightened away?

He tiptoed into the dark kitchen again to take up his post at the window. The poplar fingers were still scratching against the sill, and the clock was still ticking loudly. Unfortunately another cloud had slipped over the moon, like a soft wool muffler that held back the light except around the edges.

Freddy closed his eyes for a moment to get used to the darkness. Then he stared toward the orchard. Sure enough, the ghost was still there! He could see the light-colored figure moving behind the trees. Moving toward the potato patch!

Slowly, gracefully, the ghost glided out into the open. And for the first time Freddy got a good look—as good a look as the dim moonlight would permit.

"Whewww," he said to himself. "If it was closer to Christmas, I'd think it was one of . . . But, of course, it couldn't be. How could it?"

60

The Ghost in the Orchard

Suddenly, for no apparent reason except curiosity, the ghost began to glide toward the open mouth of the barn. It walked lightly, as if the earth were made of air and feathers. Freddy heard his heart jumping around in his ears again. He opened and closed his hands. If the ghost went into the barn . . . maybe . . . maybe, Freddy thought, he could slip out quietly and close the garage doors. Maybe he could catch the ghost!

In front of the open hole of darkness the ghost paused, holding its headdress high. Then it walked into the mouth of shadows.

Freddy gasped. There was no time to be afraid! He knew he would have to move quickly and quietly. If he went out the back way, he might make too much noise. So, trembling with excitement, he hurried to the living room and slipped out the front door.

Underfoot the short-clipped sod was soft and quiet. Carefully he ducked around the house, keeping in the shadows. He would have to make a break for the barn, after leaving the last shadow. What if the ghost tried to rush out before Freddy could shut both doors?

Freddy darted forward. Quickly he closed one door. Then the other! He felt hot all over, although the night was chilly and he had come out without a coat. "Whewww," he sighed. He had caught a ghost!

Back in the house Freddy looked at the clock. Nine fifteen. He would have to hurry if he was to get to bed by 9:30, the way Mom expected. But he would have to warn Pop not to put the car in the

61

barn. How could he? A sign! That was it. He would print a sign and tack it to the garage doors.

He took the cardboard from the back of his school tablet and a piece of black crayon and wrote "WARNING." Then he stopped. How did you spell *ghost*? He knew there was an H in it somewhere, but where? Well, there wasn't time to look it up. He bent over the cardboard:

WARNING!

GOHST INSIDE

DO NOT OPEN THE DOORS

Then he found some tacks in the nail box, and went out to put up the sign.

After a night of tossing and turning, Freddy woke up when he heard Mom and Pop stirring about in the kitchen. The first thing he did was to look out the window. Good! The car was parked in front of the barn. The doors were still closed and the sign still in place. The ghost . . . but, now that it was daylight, Freddy wasn't so sure about the ghost. He wondered if he had dreamed it, after all.

"What's all this nonsense about not opening the garage doors?" Pop asked when Freddy came into the kitchen.

"And what is a G-O-H-S-T?" asked Mom, standing by the stove watching the toast. "Did you walk in your sleep? I *told* you not to eat too much cake last night."

The little girls looked from Freddy to Mom to Pop, wondering what it was all about. Their eyes bulged when Freddy began to tell his story . . . about the ghost in the orchard, how it went into the barn, how he sneaked out and closed the doors.

"Humph," Pop said, and came over to put his hand on Freddy's forehead. "You don't seem to have a fever, son. Stick out your tongue. Hmmm. Looks all right. What kind of ghost did you say it was?"

"Well . . . maybe it sounds crazy . . . but it looked like the ghost of something that belongs to Santa Claus."

Pop gave Freddy a queer look. "Come on out, boy. We'll have to look into this. We can go through the workshop, so we won't disturb your *ghost.*"

Ten minutes later Freddy and his father were back in the house, all excited.

"What is it?" Mom asked anxiously.

"Get the long distance operator and have her put through a call to the Denver Zoo at City Park." Pop never liked to talk on the telephone, he always made Mom do it. "We've got to talk to somebody there."

"About the ghost?"

"About the ghost," Pop answered, as Mom went to the phone. "I've got to find out if they know anything about it. It's the strangest creature I ever saw. Freddy's right. It looks like the ghost of one of

63

Santa Claus's reindeer; the kind you see in pictures. Only this one's real. It's breathing-real and alive."

"It's a little pale yellow deer with regular reindeer antlers," Freddy said.

"Not a bit like our mule-deer around here," Pop put in.

Freddy laughed. "You can see why it looked like a ghost, light colored like that, behind the trees in the orchard. Only I thought it had on a fancy hat."

Mom finally got the call through to the zoo and the right person on the other end. And before long the mystery of Freddy's ghost was all cleared up. It was a fallow deer, from England. Several fallow deer had escaped from the zoo some months before and lost themselves in the hills.

"It must have liked your apples," the man from the zoo said. "We'll be over to pick it up this afternoon. That's some boy you have, folks . . . catching a ghost single-handed!"

Misha Arenstein

MRS. ALCOTT'S VISITOR

As soon as Mary Margaret McDuel opened her bedroom door she started hearing that eerie sound again—a hum. When she cupped her hands over her ears she could still hear the sound—a long, low hum. It certainly wasn't the kind of sound that Mary Margaret McDuel had ever heard at home. It wasn't the hum a refrigerator makes. And it wasn't the soft hum of her electric clock.

No one else was in the house. Mary Margaret McDuel was visiting her aunt, who lived in Concord, Massachusetts, a town where many famous events once happened and where many famous people had lived.

Mary Margaret McDuel's aunt was a writer, a real, live author. At dinner she had said, "Mary Margaret, I hope you won't be afraid to stay alone for a few hours on your first evening here. I need to find a

65

few more facts for a story I'm writing about Louisa May Alcott. I'm sure you know who she is."

"Louisa May Alcott! She's one of my favorite authors," Mary Margaret McDuel exclaimed. "I love *Little Women.* It always makes me cry, especially the part when Beth dies."

"Well," her aunt said, "Miss Alcott lived right here in Concord. Tomorrow I'll show you the house she lived in. But will you be all right alone tonight? You can go to bed early and read if you like."

And that is exactly what Mary Margaret McDuel did! She had a spooky story, just the right kind for this old house. But the story was a mistake. It scared her so that she began to hear every sound—leaves blowing outside, a cat howling, even a shutter rattling outside her window.

At long last she felt sleepy and closed her eyes. That's when she heard the hum—a low, steady hum—never louder, never softer.

Something had to be done, she decided. She couldn't hide under the covers and imagine things. There were rooms downstairs in this house that she hadn't even glanced into. Perhaps the hum was coming from one of them.

Mary Margaret McDuel put on her slippers, tied her robe around her waist, and carefully felt her way downstairs. She was mad at herself for not being able to find the light switch, but made her way to the kitchen safely. Maybe a glass of milk would help. But her hands shook as she took the milk carton from the refrigerator.

66

This just won't do, she said to herself. She looked at the kitchen clock. It was a little after ten. Her aunt should be home soon.

The humming sound continued. She couldn't shut it out. A prickle of fear ran down her back. She tiptoed from the dining room to the living room. The sound was definitely not coming from either room.

Still tiptoeing, she moved down the dark hall. Upstairs the light from her room shone comfortingly. She felt for the hall light switch, but couldn't locate it.

Holding her breath, she inched along the hall until she came to an open door. She glimpsed a patch of moonlight on the bare wooden floor. Here, the hum was louder. It seemed to be drawing her into the room.

An old rocking chair was near the door. Was it moving? She felt sure someone was sitting in the chair. She had to make herself look. Then she saw an old shawl draped over the back of the chair; it had fooled her. The rocker was empty.

The hum was loud. Mary Margaret McDuel looked desperately around. The bright moonlight made everything a pale, unearthly color. A white face suddenly seemed to look right at Mary Margaret. She was too frightened to scream—and then she realized she was staring at her own reflection in a mirror.

Just then Mary Margaret McDuel heard a sound she knew. It was her aunt's car turning into the driveway beside the house.

67

Without a backward glance, Mary Margaret McDuel ran out of the empty room and down the dark hall toward the door.

A key scraped in the lock and the door was pushed open. Mary Margaret McDuel heard her aunt give a quick gasp.

"Mary Margaret! You scared me. What are you doing down here? You look like a ghost!"

"Maybe it's because—maybe because there is a ghost here," Mary Margaret said in a rush.

"Here?" asked her aunt. "Nonsense. But something has scared you. What is it?"

Mary Margaret McDuel began to feel a little foolish. It was silly to think about ghosts. And it didn't sound very convincing as she told her aunt, "I kept hearing a hum. A constant humming sound. It wasn't very loud. It never seemed to change. I was just trying to find it when you came home."

Mary Margaret McDuel led her aunt down the hall and stopped. "Listen," she said. "Can you hear it? I haven't made it up."

"Oh!" exclaimed her aunt. "I can solve that mystery for you. That hum is my electric typewriter. I must have forgotten to turn it off when I finished typing this afternoon. That's pretty careless of me."

She hurried over to her desk, turned off the switch, and the hum immediately stopped.

"Your typewriter?" said Mary Margaret McDuel. "Well, I feel silly about this whole thing, still I'm glad that's all it was. But this

68

room looked so ghostly, with the moonlight shining in and that shawl on the rocking chair. I was sure someone was sitting there, humming to somebody else in the room. I guess my imagination got carried away."

"Someone sitting and humming?" her aunt asked. She walked slowly behind the rocking chair to a small round table. She lifted a pale blue china cup and saucer from the table.

"Isn't *this* strange?" she said more to herself than to Mary Margaret.

"What?" Mary Margaret McDuel asked. "What's strange?"

"This cup and saucer here. It's as if this is part of this town's real history."

Mary Margaret McDuel pulled her robe around her tighter and then her aunt said quickly, "Let's go back to the kitchen and have some milk and cookies. I'll tell you what's supposed to have happened right here in Concord."

Now the house seemed cozy, and Mary Margaret McDuel got ready to listen.

"People in Concord do, or at least did, believe in ghosts," her aunt began. "As a matter of fact, Louisa May Alcott probably half-believed in one particular ghost. The Alcotts, you see, moved into the house once owned by the Thoreaus."

Mary Margaret was a bit confused, so her aunt said, "You'll read about Henry David Thoreau sometime. Neighbors thought he behaved in an odd fashion, but his mother was worse. She was a strong-minded old woman who expected everyone to listen to what she said. She always had the last word about everything."

"Was that long ago?" asked Mary Margaret.

"About a hundred years ago. Anyway, Mrs. Thoreau considered herself a good friend of the Alcotts and especially of Louisa May's mother. She'd come and rock and share a cup of tea with Mrs. Alcott, never taking off her poke bonnet."

"This doesn't sound very much like a ghost story," Mary Margaret McDuel said.

"Wait. Time went by, and Mrs Alcott in her old age became ill and needed a great deal of care. Louisa May had her hands full. She was glad when she had a chance to hire a young girl who had just come from Scotland. When the girl's first day of work was over, Louisa May took her upstairs to a small room in an ell at the back of the house. 'It's a warm night,' she told her. 'Leave your door open so you can get some air. No one else is in this part of the house. If you hear a noise or see a light, pay no attention. It is just someone looking after my mother.' So in a house that was still strange to her, the girl tried to fall asleep."

Mary Margaret shivered. She knew just how that girl must have felt.

"The girl lay in bed and finally fell asleep. An old clock striking in the silent house awakened her. She looked toward the open door of

70

her room. A light seemed to be coming along the hall, drifting toward her, as if someone was climbing up the stairs.

"The figure of a woman dressed in a shawl and old-fashioned bonnet entered the room. The girl was too terrified to scream. Paying no attention whatsoever to the girl in the bed, the figure moved around the room. Carrying a flickering candle, it seemed to be looking around for something, but found nothing.

"At last, ready to leave, the figure turned toward the bed. In horror, the girl saw that the bonnet was empty. No face! No head! Just an empty bonnet faced the bed. Silently, then, the shawled creature withdrew, appeared to open a door in the hall, and descend an invisible flight of stairs."

"No face? No head?" exclaimed Mary Margaret, her heart skipping a beat. "What happened next?"

"Nothing. The girl was too frightened to venture out into the dark house. But when dawn came, she dressed and crept downstairs, determined never to spend another night under the Alcott roof. Miss Alcott and the cook were busy in the kitchen. They saw immediately that something was wrong. When the girl's story was finished, the cook and Miss Alcott looked at each other. They seemed surprised, yet not surprised."

"What do you mean?" asked Mary Margaret.

"They weren't surprised because the description of the bonnet and shawl fitted Mrs. Thoreau, who had lived for years in the same house

71

the Alcotts now occupied. Each night, afraid of fire, Mrs. Thoreau had always gone from room to room, carrying her candle, to be sure all was safe."

"But—but was it Mrs. Thoreau? Could it be?" Mary Margaret asked.

Her aunt paused, looked at the blue cup and saucer in front of her on the kitchen table, and said, "Earlier in Mrs. Alcott's illness, a woman had been hired to sit at her bedside throughout the night. In the morning she told Louisa May that her mother had had a late caller—a woman in bonnet and shawl came in, made herself a cup of tea, and sat beside the bed in an old rocker. She left as quietly as she came. Louisa May was positive it was Mrs. Thoreau."

"Is that all?" Mary Margaret asked with disappointment.

"All—except that Mrs. Thoreau had been dead for five years when the nurse reported the strange visitor."

Mary Margaret McDuel knew she and her aunt were sharing the same thoughts. The shawl on the chair, the cup and saucer nearby. But could a ghost from the 1870's, no matter how determined to tell her own story, turn on an electric typewriter? There was that cup and saucer though. It was weird. Too weird for words!

Bruce and Nancy Roberts

GRAY MAN'S WARNING

Mary MacLendon was nine when she came to Pawley's Island, South Carolina, to visit her grandmother and the first thing the boy next door did was to tell her about the Gray Man.

"Lots of people around here have seen him," said Jimmy, "and this is the time of year he comes."

"Why does he come this time of year?"

"Because it's the hurricane season. He appears to warn people if there's a bad storm coming. Hasn't your grandmother told you? If you see him you'd better watch out."

"You mean something will really happen?"

"It sure will. You might get washed right off this little old island and your house, too, if you don't do what he says."

73

Mary shivered. "Have you ever seen him?"

"No. They say he comes before all the bad storms but I've never been out here before a hurricane. Ask your grandmother. She'll tell you about him. I've got to go now. See you later." And Jimmy Lattimore's tanned legs took off down the beach.

Mary walked along the water's edge until she came to the high sand dunes that protected her grandmother's house from the wind and the waves. After supper while her grandmother was straightening the kitchen, Mary said, "Grandmother, do you think I will see the Gray Man while I'm here?"

"The Gray Man! Whoever told you that story? I'll bet it was that Lattimore boy. Has he ever seen him?"

"No, but he says lots of people have. Have you, Grandmother?"

"My goodness, no. And I don't expect to!"

"Well, how did the story about him get started?"

"Years ago plantation owners had their summer homes here on the island. One of the girls was engaged to a young man who had been abroad for two years and she got word he would be home soon. She and her mother began to cook his favorite food and decorate the house. On the ride from his own house to hers, the young man and a friend who was riding along the beach with him began to race. He took a short cut through a swampy place and his horse fell. When he tried to get to his feet he found he was only sinking deeper into the mud. His friend tried to help him but it was too late.

74

"The girl was so sad she would walk for hours up and down the beach. Then late one afternoon she saw a man standing looking out over the water. He was dressed in gray, and when she saw him clearly she was sure it was her fiancé. She ran over toward him, but when she was just a few feet away, a cloud of mist swirled up from the sea around him and he disappeared.

"That night she dreamed she was in a tiny boat with big waves all around her. She could hear people screaming and see pieces of houses floating past. When she told her parents the next morning they decided to take her to a doctor in Charleston that very afternoon.

"A little while after they left the island, a terrible hurricane hurled itself upon the coast. Houses were swept out to sea before anyone could escape, and many people living along the water died in the storm. By now the girl and her parents knew that seeing the Gray Man and her dream that night had saved their lives. And that's how the story of the Gray Man started."

Mary stayed with her grandmother all summer. Day after day she jumped the waves, liking the way it felt as the water sucked at the sand beneath her toes. She dug into the wet sand catching sand fleas and she collected shells.

A few days before she was to leave she went out on the raised walkway after supper. A man was walking along the beach. He was dressed in gray from head to toe. Mary started down the dune toward him and as she did he looked up at her. There was something about him that sent a chill down Mary's back but she made up her mind to see who he was. He walked along swinging his arms, and she didn't know whether he had seen her. Perhaps she could catch up with him if she cut across one of the dunes.

When she reached the top, there he stood over near the water. But even as she stared at him he began to grow dim. Mary forgot to be afraid and began to race down the sand toward the water. It was too late for by now he was only a grayish blur and in a moment was gone. She was alone on the beach.

Gray Man's Warning

Mary was sure she had seen the Gray Man. And if the Gray Man appeared then a hurricane was on the way. She ran back to the house wondering whether her grandmother would believe her or not. While she was telling her about the gray figure on the beach Jimmy Lattimore's father came to their door.

"Mrs. MacLendon, we've just gotten word there's a bad storm off the coast headed this way. Can we take you and Mary into Georgetown to your house there?"

"You certainly can. We'll be packed in a few minutes," said her grandmother, and they were soon on their way. That night the wind

and the rain battered at their house in Georgetown and the rain was not over until early the next morning.

Mr. Lattimore came over to see if they would like to go out to the island with him. Everyone wanted to see what had happened. They heard many homes were full of water and sand and had been badly damaged by the storm.

When Mary and her grandmother reached their house they were very surprised. The doll's suitcase Mary had forgotten and left half open on the steps was still there. It hadn't been washed or blown away. There was no water or sand inside the house. And everything Mary had hung on the line across the porch the afternoon before was still there. Not even one towel had been blown away by the terrible winds of the hurricane!

Mary's grandmother looked at her and shook her head. She just couldn't believe everything was all right.

"You really must have seen the Gray Man, child. I've always heard that when he appears to someone, the storm never touches their home." Then Grandmother MacLendon had to sit down in the rocker and just rock and look out of the window for a while.

Elizabeth Yates

THE FRIENDLY GHOST

Julie had never been away from home before and her first night in the country was a frightening one. Of course, she knew Aunt Anna and Uncle Harry well for they had often come to the city to visit her parents. But this was the first time she had been at the farm and Julie wasn't at all sure that she was going to like making friends with horses and cows and chickens. She wished she hadn't come. She wished she could go home tomorrow. She wished—Julie put her hands up to her eyes. She didn't want to cry. She was nine years old now and that was much too old to cry, but she did feel lonely and strange as she stood in the middle of her room before she got ready for bed.

There was a knock at the door. "May I come in, Julie? I've got something for you." It was Uncle Harry's cheerful voice.

"Ye-es," Julie said, swallowing quickly and trying to smile.

"I've brought you some apples in case you get hungry in the night." Uncle Harry set the plate with three polished red apples on it on the little table by the window. "They're the first of the crop. I just picked them today. Aren't they beauties?"

"Ye-es," Julie said.

"Aren't you going to undress soon?"

"Ye-es," Julie said.

Uncle Harry looked out the window of the small ground-floor bedroom. "I used to have this room when I was a boy," he said. "I always liked it because I could watch the horses and cows in the pasture. How would you like to ride one of the horses sometime, Julie?"

Julie clapped her hands together. "I'd like that."

Uncle Harry nodded. "Ned is the steadiest one, but Daisy is all right if she likes you."

"How would I know if she likes me?"

"Oh, you'll know all right, 'cause she'll come right up to you of her own accord."

After Uncle Harry left the room, Julie began to think that life in the country might not be so lonely after all. She undressed quickly and had just got into bed when Aunt Anna came in to say good night.

80

The Friendly Ghost

It was a mild August night but it would be cooler by morning, Aunt Anna said as she tucked the little girl in and leaned over to kiss her.

"Sleep well, darling, and don't be alarmed if you hear noises in the night. An old house creaks now and then."

"Why?" Julie asked, holding tight to Aunt Anna's hand as she did not want her to go.

"It's just the way the boards have of talking to themselves, telling about the things they've seen."

"Does it mean there are ghosts?"

"Mercy no, child," Aunt Anna laughed. "Whoever put such an idea in your head?"

But long after Aunt Anna left the room, Julie wondered about that. She lay wide awake in the darkness, and the air coming in the window near the head of her bed ruffled the white curtains. Outside there were crickets chirping and katydids singing, but inside everything was quiet—or almost quiet.

Now and then a board in the floor gave out a small sound and another one in the wall would answer it. Julie shut her eyes tight, not wanting to see what might be in her room, but quite sure that something was.

A cold little shiver began to run down her spine, for all the world as if someone had taken a dipper of water from the bucket by the well and poured it down her back. Julie opened her eyes for a moment, daring herself to look, but in the darkness she could see nothing. She wished that morning would come soon, and then she thought that she would eat one of the apples Uncle Harry had put on the table by her bed.

She sat up and reached out her hand, but just as she did so she heard a thump outside the window. And then, right in front of her eyes, she could see the curtains at the window move, very slowly, while something long and thin and white reached into the room, across the table by the window. Julie screamed and pulled the bedclothes over her. Then she dived down to the foot of the bed.

Aunt Anna and Uncle Harry heard the muffled screams of the little girl and came running down the stairs. They switched on the light in Julie's room and threw back the bedcovers.

"It was a ghost, I know it was," Julie said, her teeth chattering as she tried to tell them what had happened.

Aunt Anna comforted her and said there weren't any such things as ghosts except in people's imaginations.

Uncle Harry laughed easily. "Well, I guess I know one little girl who shouldn't eat apples before she goes to sleep."

"But I d-didn't eat an apple," Julie insisted. "I was just g-going to."

"That's funny," Uncle Harry said, "for I'm sure I put three apples on the plate and now there are only two."

Aunt Anna stared at the plate. "Perhaps you ate one yourself, Harry, for I certainly polished three apples."

82

Julie looked longest of anyone at the plate. "I know I didn't eat one," she said.

It was decided that Aunt Anna should sleep with Julie the rest of the night. She slipped into the big bed beside the little girl and cuddled her close. They whispered for a while together until they both began to feel sleepy.

Suddenly Julie pressed Aunt Anna's hand tightly. "What's that?"

"Just a board in the floor," Aunt Anna answered drowsily. "You'll get used to sounds like that in an old house."

Julie felt comforted, though she did not close her eyes again for a while. Instead she watched the curtains fluttering at the window. She was not afraid now because she knew that if that long white Thing reached in through the window she could waken Aunt Anna and the two of them could send it away.

But nothing happened and before long Julie fell asleep.

At breakfast, they all laughed about the strange visitor. Even Julie found it quite easy to joke about ghosts in daylight. Uncle Harry said it must have been a dream, and Aunt Anna said it was probably Julie's imagination. But neither of them could explain why, when there had been three apples on the plate, there were only two left.

Aunt Anna settled it for herself finally by saying, "You must have eaten one in your sleep, dear."

Julie shook her head. If she had, where were the core and the seeds?

83

That first day in the country was an active one for Julie. She helped Aunt Anna in the house and then she helped Uncle Harry outdoors, feeding the chickens and picking up apples in the orchard. She sat on the pasture bars and watched the two farm horses, wondering when Uncle Harry would let her ride one of them. She liked brown Ned, but it was the white mare Daisy who had Julie's heart. In the afternoon, Julie went berrying with Aunt Anna. By the time evening came she was so full of sun and August wind and good times that she was quite ready for bed.

Aunt Anna said to Julie, "No ghosts tonight, dear. If you do see or hear anything, remember that it's just the wind at the window or the old boards in the house."

Julie was too tired to think about ghosts and far too happy. She lay in bed with her eyes almost closed, remembering all the wonderful things she had done that day. When a board creaked in the floor, she smiled to herself and thought how friendly it was to have a house so old that it could speak to one. She thought perhaps if she listened long enough that she would be able to tell what it was saying and then she would talk back. But she was much too sleepy tonight to do that.

And then, suddenly, she wasn't sleepy any more and her eyes that had been half shut were wide open. The curtain began to move at the window and the long white Thing that she had seen the night before came into the room.

84

Julie didn't waste any time screaming. She simply shot under the bedcovers and pulled them down around her at the foot of the bed. Whatever the Thing was, she had seen it with her eyes and she was afraid that the next minute it would speak to her. She hardly dared move under the covers. But she decided not to take any chances and she did not put her head out until morning.

When Aunt Anna came in to wake Julie, she found her sleeping like a rabbit in its burrow, curled up at the foot of the bed with the sheets and the blankets all higgledy-piggledy.

Julie told her what had happened. "It was a ghost," she whispered. "I know it was."

Aunt Anna laughed right out loud. "You are a silly little girl. You ought to know that there aren't any such things as ghosts, not in this house anyway."

And then she looked at the plate on the table by the bed and smiled. "Why, Julie, you've eaten another apple! Uncle Harry will be glad that you like them so much."

Julie looked at the table for the first time that morning and her eyes grew as round as saucers.

The plate had only one apple left on it.

There were pancakes for breakfast and, somehow, laughing and talking with her aunt and uncle, the mystery of the night began to seem rather far away from Julie.

That afternoon, Uncle Harry took Julie by the hand and they

went to the gateway together. He called to the two horses and when they came up to him he slipped their bridles on and asked Julie which one she would rather ride.

"I'd like to ride Daisy," Julie said.

Uncle Harry shook his head. "Daisy doesn't make friends easily, but perhaps she'll be all right with you."

He lifted Julie up on to the mare's broad back. Then he got on brown Ned and together they ambled off to round up the cows for the milking. Uncle Harry nodded his head in surprise when he saw how gentle the horse was with the young girl from the city.

"I guess you've been making up to my old Daisy on the quiet," he said.

Julie shook her head and ran her hand down Daisy's neck. She was glad that Uncle Harry wouldn't have to think she was scared of everything, for the shuddering things that had been happening at night had made her a little ashamed of herself.

That night Julie went bravely to bed. Aunt Anna offered to sleep downstairs with her, but Julie said she would rather not. She felt quite certain now that she must have been dreaming for she knew there couldn't be any ghosts in a house as nice as the one her aunt and uncle lived in. Nobody believed her when she said she hadn't eaten the apples. So puzzled was Julie by their disappearance that she had begun to wonder if perhaps she had eaten them in her sleep—cores, seeds, and all.

86

"Good night, Julie dear, and I hope you won't have any dreams at all tonight," Aunt Anna said.

Julie was so tired and happy that she didn't spend any time at all lying awake and thinking. Instead she went sound asleep; nor would she have awakened before morning if sometime during the night she had not heard a curious sound. Feeling something warm near her face, she opened her eyes.

Moonlight was filling the room and in its soft glow Julie could see clearly that something had thrust its head in the window. She sat up in bed and a lump of fear rose right into the middle of her throat. She opened her mouth to scream, to call out for her aunt and uncle. Then suddenly she saw who it was: Daisy!

Julie put out her hand and stroked the long white head. Then she ran her fingers over the velvet nostrils that had bent so near her that she could feel the warm breath coming through them.

"Hello, Daisy," she said softly. "That was a nice ride we had, wasn't it? I hope we can have one like that every day."

Daisy tossed her head and gave a little neigh.

Julie wished she had a lump of sugar to give the horse, but she explained to Daisy that she would bring one to the gateway the next morning.

"Do you like apples?" she asked, remembering that there was one left on the plate.

But when she looked at the plate she saw that it was empty!

87

Slowly a wide smile spread over Julie's face, "I guess you *do* like apples," she said.

Daisy drew her head back from the window and whinnied. Then she flicked her back feet and Julie saw her trotting across the grass, taking the low pasture bars in her stride.

Uncle Harry and Aunt Anna could scarcely believe what Julie had to tell them the next morning at breakfast. But when they went out and saw the hoof marks on the grass, from the window up to the pasture bars, they had to admit that Julie's ghost was only a friendly visitor who liked apples as much as she liked the girl from the city.

Once-upon-a-time
GHOSTS

GHOST STORY

One night close to my nose
Something crept by on tippy-toes.
It went swish, swash, and whoo-whoo-ee,
and it sure scared Joe and me.

But then it said, "I cannot stay,
I must be off and away.
I'm very late
for an important date."
We weren't sorry to see it go,
me and Joe.

Lisl Weil

Maria Leach
HERE WE GO!

Once there was a rich farmer who had a fine farm, fine horses and cattle, a fine big house, and a fine wife and several children. He was a very happy man—happy, that is, except for one thing. There was a boggart in the house.

Boggart is a north-of-England word for a kind of trick-playing spirit which takes up its abode in people's houses and barns. Some say it is a ghost, and some say it is just a mischief-maker. It never really hurts anyone, but it can play a lot of painful practical jokes.

This farmer and his wife had a boggart. It used to walk around in the house at night and pull the covers off of people. It used to knock on the door and when the sleepy farmer got up and went downstairs to open it, there would be nobody there.

92

It used to fall downstairs in the dark, making an awful racket, and when the wife ran into the hall, fearing it was one of the children, all the children would be safely asleep in bed.

Sometimes it would just tap, tap, tap in the night on the lid of the linen chest. Sometimes it would roll a heavy ball across the floor, time and again, so no one could sleep, or let it go bump-bumping down the stairs. One night it threw all the pots and pans down the cellar stairs. That was a clatter!

Once in a while the boggart would pitch in and help the family. It would wash the dishes when the farmer's wife wasn't looking; or sometimes it would churn the butter or collect the eggs. It would feed and water the cows and horses. But more often than not it would tie knots in their tails or let them loose in the night so the farmer had to go looking for them. Once it broke all the cups and saucers.

One of its favorite tricks was to blow all the smoke back *down* the chimney whenever anyone tried to light a fire. Or it would blow out the match just when someone was trying to make a light.

At last the farmer and his wife got tired of all this. They could put up with a prank now and then. But this boggart was so annoying and troublesome that something had to be done.

So they decided to move. They decided to move to a new house on a big farm far away where there would be no boggarts.

The man and his wife and children packed up all their belongings and piled them high on the big wagon.

Just as they were about to drive off, a neighbor came by and said, "Oh, are you moving?"

"Yes," said the man. He explained that the boggart's tricks had at last become unbearable. They could not stand their boggart any longer, so they were moving.

So the neighbor wished them luck, and they drove off. Then from the top of the load they heard a little voice say happily, "Well, here we go! We're off!"

Sorche Nic Leodhas

THE HOUSE THAT LACKED A BOGLE

There once was a house that lacked a bogle. That would be no great thing for a house to be wanting in the ordinary way, but it happened that this house was in St. Andrews. That being a town where every one of the best houses has a ghost or a bogle, as they call it, of its own, or maybe two or even more, the folks who lived in the house felt the lack sorely. They were terribly ashamed when their friends talked about their bogles, seeing that they had none of their own.

The worst of it was that they had but lately come into money and had bought the house to set themselves up in the world. They never thought to ask if it had a bogle when they bought it, just taking it for

95

granted that it had. But what good was it to be having a fine big house if there was no bogle in it? In St. Andrews anyway!

The man of the house could be reckoned a warm man with a tidy lot of money at his banker's, while his neighbor MacParlan had a hard time of it scraping enough to barely get by. But the MacParlans had a bogle that had been in the family since the time of King Kenneth the First, and they had papers to prove it.

The woman of the house had two horses to her carriage, and Mrs. MacNair had no carriage at all. But the MacNairs had *three* bogles, being well supplied, and Mrs. MacNair was so set up about them that it fair put one's teeth on edge to hear her going on about them and their doings.

Tammas, the son of the house, told his parents that he couldn't hold up his head when chaps talked about their bogles at his school, and he had to admit that there weren't any at this house at all.

And then there was Jeannette, the daughter of the house (her name was really Janet but she didn't like the sound of it, its being so plain). Well, *she* came home one day, and banged the door to, and burst into tears. And when they all asked her what was amiss, she said she'd been humiliated entirely because they hadn't a bogle, and she'd never show her face outside the house again until her papa got one for her.

Well, it all came to this. Without a bogle, they could cut no figure at all in society, for all their money.

They did what they could, of course, to set the matter right. In

96

fact, each one of them tried his own way, but not letting on to the others, however, lest they be disappointed if naught came of it.

The man of the house kept an eye on MacParlan's house and found out that MacParlan's bogle liked to take a stroll by nights on the leads of MacParlan's roof. So one night, when all the MacParlans had gone off somewhere, he went over and called up to MacParlan's bogle. After a bit of havering, the man got down to the point. "Do you not get terrible tired of haunting the same old place day in and day out?" he asked.

"What way would I be doing that?" the bogle asked, very much surprised.

"Och, 'twas just a thought I had," said the man. "You might be liking to visit elsewhere maybe?"

"That I would not," said the bogle flatly.

"Och well," said the man, "should you e'er feel the need o' a change of scene, you'll find a warm welcome at my house any time and for as long as you're liking to stay."

The bogle peered down at him over the edge of the roof.

"Thank you kindly," said he, "but I'll bide here wi' my own folks. So dinna expect me." And with that he disappeared.

So there was naught for the man to do but go back home.

The woman of the house managed to get herself asked to the MacNairs' house for tea. She took with her a note to the MacNairs' bogles, telling them she was sure the three of them must be a bit cramped for room, what with there being so many of them and the MacNairs' house being so small. So she invited any or all of them to come over and stay at her house, where they'd find plenty of room and every comfort provided that a bogle could ever wish.

When nobody was watching, she slipped the note down behind the wainscoting in the MacNairs' drawing room, where she was sure the MacNairs' bogles would be finding it.

The MacNairs' bogles found it all right, and it surprised them. They didn't know exactly what to make of the note when they'd read it. But there was no doubt the woman meant it kindly, they said to each other. Being very polite bogles, they decided that she deserved the courtesy of an answer to the note, and since none of them was very much for writing, the least they could do was to send one of themselves to decline the invitation. The woman had paid them a call, so to speak. So one of them went to attend to it that same night.

The bogle met up with the woman of the house just as she was coming out of the linen press with a pile of fresh towels in her arms. The maids had left that day, being unwilling to remain in a house so inferior that it had no bogle to it. She'd have been startled out of her wits had she not been so glad to see the bogle.

"Och then!" said she, "'tis welcome you are entirely!"

"Thank ye kindly," said the bogle.

"You'll be stopping here I hope?" questioned the woman eagerly.

98

"I'm sorry to be disappointing you," said the bogle, "but I'm not staying. I'm needed at home."

"Och now," said the woman, "and could they not make do without you just for a month or two? Or happen even a fortnight?"

But she could see for herself that the bogle was not to be persuaded. In fact, none of them could accept her invitation. That's what the bogle had come to tell her. With their thanks, of course.

"'Tis a sore thing," complained the woman, "what with all the money paid out for the house and all, that we have no bogle of our own. Now can you be telling me why?"

"I would not like to say," said the bogle.

But the woman was sure he knew the reason, so she pressed him until at last the bogle said reluctantly, "Well, this is the way of it. The house is too young! Losh! 'Tis not anywhere near a hundred years old yet, and there's not been time enough for anything to have happened that would bring it a bogle of its own. And forebye . . ." The bogle stopped talking at that point.

"Och! What more?" urged the woman.

"We-e-ell," said the bogle slowly, "I'd not be liking to hurt your feelings, but your family is not, so to speak, distinguished enough. Now you take the MacParlans and the MacPhersons and the MacAlistairs—their families go back into the far ages. And the MacAlpines is as old as the hills and rocks and streams. As for the MacNairs," he added proudly, "och, well the MacNairs *is*

99

the MacNairs. The trouble with your family is that there is nothing of note to it. No one knows exactly where it would be belonging. There's no clan or sept o' the name. Losh! The name has not even a 'Mac' at the front of it."

"Aye," said the woman slowly, "I can see that fine."

And so she could. For the truth was that they had come from Wigtown and were not a Highland family at all.

"Well," said the bogle, "that's the way it is. So I'll bid you good night." And away he went like a drift of mist, leaving the poor woman of the house alone and uncomforted.

The daughter of the house had taken to her bed and spent her time there, weeping and sleeping, when she wasn't eating sweeties out of a pink satin box and reading romantic tales about lovely ladies who had adventures in castles just teeming with ghosts and handsome gentlemen in velvet suits of clothes.

So there was no one left to have a try but the son, Tammas. It must be admitted he did the best he could, even if it turned out that he was maybe a little bit too successful.

Tammas had got to the place where he kept out of the way of his friends on account of the shame that was on the family, he being young and full of pride. He only went out by night, taking long walks in lonely places all by himself.

One night he was coming back from one of these walks, and he came along by a kirkyard. It was just the sort of spot that suited his

100

gloomy thoughts, so he stopped and leaned over the wall to look at the long rows of gravestones.

"All those graves lying there," he thought, "with many a bogle from them stravaging through the town and not a one of them for us. 'Tis not fair on us."

He stopped to think about the injustice of it, and then he said out loud, "If there's a bogle amongst you all who's got no family of his own, let him just come along with me. He can bide with us and be welcome." And with a long, deep sigh he turned back up the road and started for home.

He'd not gone more than twenty paces past the end of the kirkyard, when all of a sudden he heard a fearful noise behind him. It was so eerie that it near raised the hair right off his head. It sounded like a cat yowling and a pig squealing and a horse neighing and an ox bellowing all at one and the same time.

Tammas scarcely dared turn and look, with the fright that was on him, but turn he did. And he saw 'twas a man coming toward him. He was dressed in Highland dress with kilt and sporran, jacket and plaid showing plain, and the moonlight glinting off his brooch and shoe buckles and off the handle of the dirk in his hose. He carried a set of bagpipes under his arm and that was where the noise was coming from.

"Whisht, man," called Tammas, "leave off with the pipes now. The racket you're making's enough to wake the dead."

101

"Twill do no such thing," said the piper. "For they're all awake already and about their business. As they should be, its being midnight."

And he put his mouth at the pipes to give another blow.

"Och, then ye'll wake all the folks in St. Andrews," protested Tammas. "Give over now, that's a good lad!"

"Och, nay," said the piper soothingly. "St. Andrew folks will pay us no heed. They're used to us. They even like us."

By this time he had come up to Tammas where he stood in the middle of the road. Tammas took another look at him to see who the piper was. And losh, 'twas no man at all. 'Twas a bogle!

" 'Tis a strangely queer thing," said the piper sadly. "I've been blowin' on these doomed things all the days of my mortal life till I plain blew the life out o' my body doing it. And I've been blowing on them two or three hundred years since then, and I just cannot learn how to play a tune on them."

"Well, go blow somewhere else," Tammas told him. "Where it's lonelylike, with none to hear you."

"I'd not be liking that at all," said the piper. "Besides, I'm coming along with you."

"With me!" Tammas cried in alarm.

"Och aye," said the piper, and then he added reproachfully. "You asked me, you know. Did you not?"

"I suppose I did," Tammas admitted reluctantly. "But I'd no idea

102

there'd be anyone there listening."

"Well *I* was there," the piper said, "and I was listening. I doubt that I'm the only bogle in the place without a family of my own. So I accept the invitation, and thank ye kindly. Let's be on our way."

And off he stepped, with his kilt swinging and his arms squared just so and the pipes going at full blast.

Tammas went along with him, because there was nowhere else he could go at that hour but back to his home.

When they got home, Tammas opened the door and into the house the two of them went. All the family came running to see what was up, for the pipes sounded worse indoors than out since there was less room there for the horrible noise to spread.

"There!" Tammas shouted at them all, raising his voice over the racket of the bagpipes. "There's your bogle for you, and I hope you're all satisfied!"

And he stomped up the stairs and into his room, where he went to bed with his pillow pulled over his ears.

Strange to tell, they really were satisfied, because now they had a bogle and could hold their own when they went out into society. Quite nicely as it happened, for they had the distinction of being the only family in the town that had a piping ghost—even if he didn't know how to play the pipes.

It all turned out very well, after all. The daughter of the house married one of the sons of the MacNairs and changed her name back to Janet, her husband liking it better. And she had a "Mac" at the front of her name at last, as well as her share of the three MacNair bogles, so she was perfectly happy.

The mother and father grew a bit deaf with age, and the piping didn't trouble them at all.

But Tammas decided he'd had all he wanted of bogles and of St. Andrews as well. So he went off to London where he made his fortune and became a real Sassenach. In time, he even got a "Sir" before his name, which gave him a lot more pleasure than he'd ever have got from a "Mac."

The bogle never did learn to play the bagpipes, though he never left off trying. But nobody cared about that at all. Not even the bogle.

Moritz Jagendorf

THE STUBBORNEST MAN IN MAINE
A NEW ENGLAND GHOST STORY

There lived a rich man near Booth Bay in Maine who was the stubbornest man in all the state.

His name was Bill Greenleaf, and when he made up his mind about something nobody could outargue him. He was as stubborn as a mule. He'd say his say, and no man could make him say different. Everybody agreed that his stubbornness would only end when he went to the better world, where maybe the angels would teach him a little giving in.

One day Bill Greenleaf called his family around him and told them his time had come. Said he:

"I've called you together to tell you I don't fancy being buried in thick, black earth. I want to be buried in shiny white sand straight

106

from Davenport Bay. From Davenport Bay and no other place."
That was a fine bay quite a distance from Squirrel Island where Bill's
house stood.

"It's to be from Davenport Bay, and don't you forget it," he
repeated over and over again.

His wife promised it would be done, and Bill Greenleaf died that
very night.

At the first peep of dawn Widow Greenleaf sent a big scow with
eight strong men to Davenport Bay to bring back enough fine, shiny
white sand to bury her late husband, just as he had asked.

The day was clear, and the wind was right, but the scow was
heavy, and it was a long, long way to Davenport Bay.

Spoke Peleg who was at the front oar:

"My arms are aching. We must row this long distance only to
please a stubborn dead fellow who can't be stubborn no more. Sand's
sand if it is from Davenport Bay in Maine or out in China Bay."

Michael, who was holding the oar alongside him, agreed.

"You're right, Peleg," he said. "Can't see why we have to suffer
from Bill's stubbornness, now he's good and dead."

Moses, who was behind him, pulled hard on his oar, nodded his
head, and added:

"We needn't pay any mind to his talk no more. He can't order us
now telling us what he wants and what he don't."

"Reckon the widow won't know the difference between one

kind of sand and another. Maybe she don't care neither," added Reuben.

"Let's get the sand right from that place there," cried Jabez, a tall red-haired fellow, pointing to a little inlet right in front of them.

The others agreed at once.

They swung the heavy scow toward land, and soon the flat bottom of the vessel scraped the white sand of the shore.

The men took the shovels with a good will, worked hard, and in quick time the vessel was full of the white sand. Then they turned homeward.

Now, when they had set out in the early morning, the sun was shining and the wind was gentle. But no sooner did they begin rowing back than there was a quick turn in the weather. The sun rushed behind black clouds, the winds came wildly from the four sides of the compass, and the bay turned into a churning sea.

Reuben and Peleg, Moses and Jabez, and all the others couldn't figure out how it came about, for there had been no sign or warning of a storm.

Rowing was hard. The big, heavy, flat-bottomed scow just wouldn't go at all. It lurched and bobbed like a sailor on a spree. At first the sand in the scow flew about in the faces and eyes of the men. Then waves began pouring in over the sides. The rain came down and made the sand brown and soggy and heavy as lead.

The storm raged worse and worse. The rain was whipping, the

wind was screeching. The men in the scow were wet and weary and madder than hornets.

Suddenly they saw through the rain a big figure flapping ghostlike.

It was swaying with the squalls, coming nearer and nearer to the boat. The rowing men turned as white as the foam that topped the waves. They stopped dead, and just held onto the sides while the scow lurched and dipped and seesawed like crazy.

The big thing was wearing a greatcoat. Nearer and nearer it came, with arms and coat flapping wildly in the tempest. Now it was near enough for all to see a stubborn white face sticking out from the big white collar.

And whose face do you think it was!

Jabez roared louder than the racing wind:

"It's old Bill Greenleaf come back!"

He could say no more. His mouth and throat were so dry that all the water in the bay and all the rain from the sky couldn't take away the dryness. The other men felt no better. They were too scared to say a word.

But Bill Greenleaf had plenty to say:

"Aye, you guessed right! Trying to cheat me just because you think I'm dead and gone. I'm dead, all right, but I ain't gone yet."

He flapped his arms and bellowed like thunder:

"Take warning! Dump that mud-sand and row down and get a scowful of Davenport Bay sand just as I stipulated. In Davenport

Bay sand I'm going to be buried and no other, mind. And don't take no year of Sundays but do it quick or I'll send you down so deep in the bay you'll drown for all your life."

There was a fast streak of lightning in the sky right then, and just as fast were Jabez, Peleg, Moses, Reuben, and the others dumping shovelfuls of sand into the bay. It wasn't sweet work, for the sand was heavy as rocks, but the men never noticed it.

Old Bill Greenleaf, swaying in the wind, looked on and never said another word.

Funny thing, the less sand there was in the scow, the quieter the wind was over the water and . . . the thinner Bill Greenleaf became.

When the scow was empty and no speck of sand left in it, Bill Greenleaf was gone—and so was the storm.

The men in the scow never said a word. Maybe it was because they were tired, or maybe they thought doing was better than talking. They rowed with all their might to Davenport Bay and loaded the sand fast as a barn a-burning. They rowed back just as fast, loaded the sand in carts, and brought it back to bury Bill Greenleaf.

That's why people still say Bill Greenleaf is the stubbornest man in all of Maine. For in no other state did anyone ever hear of a man who was as stubborn when he was dead as when he was alive.

110

Lupe de Osma

THE DANCING JUG

Once upon a time, there lived in a village up in the mountains a man possessed by a terrible sin. He loved money better than anything else in the world. He had more pesos than he could count; but the more he had, the more he wanted, and he spent his days grasping and pinching every penny he could.

And as soon as he had a bagful of pesos he would exchange them for coins of pure gold. These he would put into a big clay jug, the kind some goodwives use to carry their water from the spring.

And his nights he spent sitting by the light of a candle, with the golden coins piled high on a table in front of him, enraptured by their

111

gleam and clink-clinking sound as they slipped one by one through his fingers. Ah, what a feast! What music! he thought. But because of his passion he was yellow and pinched, like a dried-up stick of wood ready for the stove.

At long last there came a day when the jug was so full of coins that it could hold no more. How his face shone with pleasure! And how he laughed, skipped, and danced for joy!

But now a problem arose for him. Where should he hide his gold? Because now he could not rest by day or sleep by night, for fear someone might steal his treasure. He thought and thought and thought—for a long time. And then one evening when the moon was not too bright, he went out into a field behind his house, looking around at every step to see that no one was watching. There, under a mango tree which stood by itself, he dug a hole and buried his jug, brimful of gold, marking the secret spot with a flat rock. Now, with his mind at ease, he went home, rubbing his hands and feeling very happy.

Well, this was all very fine for the yellow and pinched miser as long as he had his health; but one day he took a chill. His condition grew steadily worse, and in three more days his thrifty life came to an end.

And what of the gold? It remained buried under the mango tree, for he had told no one of it.

But now something new came up. Shortly after the miser's

112

funeral, there appeared one evening a curious light. A neighbor who was returning home late (it must have been midnight or thereabouts) chanced to take the path across the field where the mango tree was. Suddenly he let out a shriek and ran in terror, barefoot though he was, over brambles and pebbles. When he got home, he tumbled through the door, almost in a swoon and deathly pale. Everyone in the house jumped out of bed, asking what was the matter; and when he found his tongue, he told them how he had seen a strange greenish-blue ball of light drifting around the mango tree, and how he had stopped to look at it and heard a frightful cry.

In these small places news travels fast, and in no time the word went around that the dead miser walked as a ghost. Needless to say, from that day forward no one would go near the path after darkness fell.

Days and months passed, and when seven years had gone by the story of the light was forgotten. And now in that vicinity, a little way from the miser's house, there lived a poor lad, who was called Tomas. He was as different from the penny-pinching miser as day is from night. This poor lad earned his living by doing errands around about the village. It was very little he earned, however, and he barely managed to keep himself alive.

Now one evening when Tomas was walking home, he took the path which led through the field behind the miser's house. It was close upon midnight and there was no moon, but the night was clear

113

and the stars were bright and looked very near. By this light Tomas could see enough to follow his way and even trace faintly the outlines of some nearby roofs.

But since it was so late, all the houses were dark. There was no flickering of candles, no thin light of kerosene lamps to be seen through the open windows anywhere. Everyone in the village was in bed and asleep. Only from far off up in the hills, where some merry folk were celebrating, there came trailing down through the air the music of a marimba, and it mingled with the lonely call of a night bird.

Presently, and without the slightest warning, there appeared along the path ahead of Tomas a greenish-blue ball of light. It came slowly, steadily . . . drifting.

"Dear me," gasped Tomas, "that's no right light!" He stood in awe, wondering what would happen next. The light continued to drift, till it was almost in front of him.

In a panic, Tomas struggled to set one foot before the other. But it was no use; his feet stood still, as if nailed to the ground. And to make matters still more distressing, when he tried to cry out for help his lips would not open and his tongue cleaved to the roof of his mouth.

Well, there he stood in a panic, with his arms hanging at his sides—helpless, waiting for some dreadful apparition to pounce and knock the very life out of him. And as he stood thus, wishing he were

114

home and safe, suddenly he heard a pitiful sigh—like the sigh of a person in pain.

That was the end, Tomas thought. He fell to his knees in terror and closed his eyes, determined to see no more. But now his voice came back to him, to his surprise; and, half swooning, he managed to beg for mercy.

"Heavens! What are you?" he gasped. "What troubles you? Oh, keep away, and don't harm a poor lad that never did you hurt!"

Upon this, the ghost heaved another pitiful sigh. "I am allowed to speak," said the voice of the ghost, "only to him who speaks first to me." Then the ghost went on to tell how he would not be able to rest till he found someone willing to talk with him and dig up his pot of gold.

Tomas could not keep his eyes closed any longer, so strong was his desire to see as well as hear everything. He opened one eye, and then the other, and looked into the darkness. He saw nothing but the ball of light; though later, when he told the story, he swore he saw a white shadow floating above the greenish ball.

Finding that the light had no harm in it, he lost his terror and even ventured to offer his help, so that the poor soul might hasten to its rest.

"Then come with me, and I'll show you a big jug full of gold," said the ghost.

115

Well, Tomas found his courage again. He arose from his knees, felt for his machete (it was always by his side), and followed the ghost with steps so light that his feet hardly touched the ground. You would have thought they drifted like the ghost itself.

When they reached the mango tree, the ghost stopped and said, "Dig under this rock here and the jug full of gold is yours."

Tomas fell to digging furiously with his knife, and three feet down he found the jug.

"That was a true service," said the ghost. "Adios, good-by. . . . Now I can go to my rest."

"Adios!" answered Tomas. "God speed you, poor soul!" But he was too busy admiring his jug to notice the ghostly light drifting up into the darkness. Away it went and no one has ever seen it again to this day.

Tomas mopped the sweat from his brow and set to work to bring the jug out. But now something unexpected happened. Just as he stretched his arms to lift it out, the clay jug gave three hops and bounded out of the hole, all by itself. And as nimbly as you please, it bobbed up and down and from side to side, right before his eyes. Poor Tomas stood wonder-struck, his mouth agape. And the jug kept on dancing around him, as if amused by his bewilderment.

"Gracious! A jug that dances! That isn't at all as it should be!" he gasped. "This is an ugly business, I can see," he added. For he suddenly remembered that there was talk around the village of

116

goblins having been seen in that field. "Aha! I think the goblins are in it, and I shall soon know for certain!"

And that was exactly what ailed the jug. It was bewitched! But Tomas knew a good remedy for goblins; he had learned it from his grandmother. Quickly he took his jacket off and turned it wrong side out. The dancing jug began to hop away as if it understood what Tomas was about.

"Not so fast, my pretty!" shouted Tomas. He was not going to let his gold run away from him like that! In a twinkling he made the sign of the cross and just as quickly, he slung the jacket over the jug. No sooner was this done than the jug stopped dancing and stood as still as a clay jug should; the power of the goblins was broken. And without one bit of dread, Tomas picked it up and carried it off toward home at top speed.

When he arrived he set the jug upon a table and stretched himself out on his woven straw mat, marveling at all the strange things he had heard and seen, and wondering if perchance he were dreaming. And while turning over the thoughts in his mind, he fell asleep.

Next morning a ray of sunshine lighted up his tiny room. Tomas awoke with a jump and dashed to the table. Yes, there stood the clay jug—brimful with gold, have no doubt—as true and real as the jasmine vine winding around his window.

Lalavihari De

THE GHOST CATCHER

Now this is a very old story. It is about a young barber who did not really want to be a barber. And it is about a ghost—two ghosts.

The young barber's name was Dev. Dev didn't like being a barber. He didn't like cutting men's hair or shaving their faces. He really wanted to be a farmer.

But Dev's father was a barber. And when Dev's father died, all he left his son was his bag of barber tools—razors, scissors, brushes, combs, and a mirror. So what could Dev do? He tried to be a barber too. In those days in India, you had to do whatever your father did.

Well, Dev was a clever boy, but he wasn't a good barber. And after a while people stopped coming to him.

118

"He is not as good a barber as his father," they said.

"I'd rather be a farmer," Dev thought. "But if I have to be a barber, I will leave this town. I will go to the city where no one knows that my father was a better barber than I."

And so Dev picked up his bag of barber tools—razors, scissors, brushes, combs, and a mirror—and set off for the city.

Dev walked all morning and he walked all afternoon.

When night came, Dev sat under a willow tree to rest. The city was still a long way off, and Dev decided to spend the night under the willow tree. "Then I can start out fresh in the morning," he said to himself. Dev lay down on the ground and fell asleep at once.

As luck would have it, that very willow tree was haunted by a ghost.

Soon after Dev fell asleep, the ghost floated down from the treetop crying, "BOOOOOOO!"

Dev woke up at once. "What a bad dream," he said to himself. "I dreamed this willow tree was haunted by a ghost."

"BOOOOOOOO!" cried the ghost again. Now he was right at Dev's ear. This was not a dream! Dev had to think fast.

"Don't you come close to me, ghost," Dev said quickly. "D-Do you know what I am? I-I'm a *ghost catcher!* That's what I am! I catch ghosts and put them in my ghost bag."

And with that Dev opened his bag of barber tools and pulled up the mirror. "Here, let me show you one ghost I've caught tonight,"

119

he said. Dev held the mirror up to the ghost's face. "I think I'll put you in the bag to keep him company."

The ghost looked into the mirror—and what did he see? His own face, of course. But he didn't know that. He thought the barber really did have a ghost in the bag.

"Oh, please," begged the ghost, "don't put me in your ghost bag. I'll give you anything you want. Just let me go."

"Anything I want?" said Dev. "Then I want a bag of gold. Maybe two bags of gold."

Zip! In a wink, two bags of gold were at Dev's feet.

"Good enough," Dev said. "I promise not to put you in my bag this time. But remember, if you bother me again, into the ghost bag you go."

As soon as Dev let the mirror fall back into the bag, the ghost was gone.

Dev never did go to the city. He took some of the gold the ghost had given him and he bought himself a farm. Dev was a fine farmer. He didn't have to cut hair or shave faces anymore. But Dev kept his bag of barber tools—and that was very clever of him.

For, as luck would have it, the ghost met his cousin one day and told him everything that had happened. At the end of his story, his ghost cousin burst out laughing.

"Hoo, hoo, hoo," he laughed. "No man can catch a ghost. And there is no such thing as a ghost bag. You have been tricked."

120

"Well, go and see for yourself," the ghost said. "But don't blame me if that man puts you in his bag."

The cousin floated over to Dev's house and peeked through the window.

Dev was eating his supper. He felt a cold breeze and looked up. Another ghost! Dev ran to get his bag of tools. Quickly, he opened the bag and pulled up the mirror.

Then he held the mirror against the window and shouted, "Come on in! I'll put you in the bag too!"

The cousin took one look at the ghost in the bag and floated off as fast as he could go.

From that time on Dev lived in peace. He was clever enough to keep his bag of barber tools handy, although he never had to use them again.

Ruth Manning-Sanders

A BOX ON THE EAR

On a cold winter's day a lad went tramping to look for work. He was hungry, he was ragged, he hadn't a penny, and he tramped on till evening. It was no night to sleep under a hedge, so he went to an inn and begged for shelter. But the landlord said they were expecting a great company that night, so ragged folk were not welcome. And he turned the lad away.

Well, the lad walked on for a bit, and then he saw a big house standing back from the road.

"Maybe I'll get a night's lodging in the kitchen here for a job of work in the morning," thought he. So he opened the gate and walked up the drive.

123

But when he drew near the house, what was his surprise to see the front door flung violently open and a crowd of people rushing out: first the mistress of the house, then the master, and then all the servants, fair tumbling over each other in their hurry to get away.

The lad stepped in front of the mistress, but she dodged round him, picked up her skirts and ran off down the drive. So then the lad gave a skip and got in front of the master.

"Sir," said he, "I have a favor to ask."

"Favor!" cried the master. "This is no time to ask for favors! Can't you see we're in a hurry to leave before the ghost comes?"

"Ah, but I've come to lay the ghost for you," said the lad, bold as brass.

"If you can do that," said the master, "you shall have a bag full of gold!"

"I'd rather have a sausage to fry," said the lad, "for my stomach is empty and crying out."

"Well, well, you'll find a sausage in the kitchen," shouted the master. And he ran off down the drive and out through the gate, and away along the road to the inn, followed by all the servants.

The lad went into the house and found his way to the kitchen. There were a few embers still smouldering on the hearth; and, yes, sure enough, there was a big sausage in a dish on a shelf.

The lad was so hungry that he ate a bit of the sausage raw. Then

124

he threw wood on the hearth till the fire roared up, for he was very cold. And after that he cut the rest of the sausage into slices, and waited for the flames on the hearth to die down. When there were no more flames, but only glowing embers, he laid some slices of sausage on the embers to toast them, turning them carefully from time to time with the fire tongs.

Ah good, good! Soon he was munching a slice of hot sausage; and with a jug of beer that he found to wash down the meat—what could a lad ask more?

So, as he was munching away at that first slice, he heard a deep voice calling from out of the chimney, "I fall! I fall!"

"Fall then!" said the lad with his mouth full. "And if you fall in pieces, what do I care?"

And hardly had he said this when, *trip, trap,* down from the chimney fell the leg of a man. The leg hopped over the hot embers, and stood itself upright on the kitchen floor. But the lad took no notice. He went on munching his toasted sausage.

And very soon the voice from the chimney spoke again: "I fall! I fall!"

"Fall then!" said the lad with his mouth full.

Trip, trap! Down from the chimney fell another leg, hopped over the hot embers, and stood itself upright on the floor beside its fellow.

The lad didn't so much as turn round. He picked another slice of sausage out of the embers, and went on eating.

"I fall, I *fall*, I FALL!" came the voice from the chimney, louder and louder.

"Fall then," said the lad, biting off a huge piece of sausage. "But why make such a fuss about it?"

Trip, trap! Down from the chimney fell the body of a man, bounced over the hot embers, and set itself up on top of the two legs.

The lad didn't look round. He went on eating.

"I fall! I FALL!" wailed the voice in the chimney.

"Fall then, and look sharp about it!" said the lad with his mouth full.

Trip, trap! Down from the chimney fell two arms, hopped over the hot embers, and joined themselves on to the ghost's body.

"It only wants its head now," said the lad. He lifted another slice of sausage from the embers and crammed it into his mouth; but he didn't look round at what stood behind him.

Then a voice came out of the chimney fairly roaring: "I FALL! I FALL! I FALL!"

"Fall then, and be done!" said the lad, with his mouth full of sausage.

And no sooner had he said that, when *trip, trap,* down from the chimney bounced a man's head, hopped over the hot embers, and set itself up on the body of the ghost.

The lad turned round then, looked the ghost full in its glaring eyes, and said, "What do you want?"

126

The ghost didn't answer. It came and sat itself down by the fire close to the lad.

The lad took the tongs and lifted a slice of sausage off the embers. He was just about to eat that slice, when the ghost licked its fingers, covered its wet fingers with ashes, and smeared the ashes all over the nicely toasted piece of sausage.

"If you do that again," said the lad, "I shall box your ears!"

And he laid another slice of sausage on the embers.

But when that slice was toasted and the lad lifted it off the embers, the ghost licked its fingers again, rubbed them in the ashes, and dirtied the slice of sausage all over.

So then the lad turned and gave the ghost such a box on the ear that it tumbled over on its back.

"And that will teach you to mind your manners," said the lad.

The ghost got to its feet. It was laughing. "Little brother, thank you! I have been seven years without rest because in life I felled my father with a box on the ear. No, I could not rest until someone did the like to me. Now I have taken my payment. And so good-bye! Good-bye!"

And when it had said that, the ghost laughed again, and vanished.

The lad went on with his cooking until he had toasted and eaten the last slice of sausage. Then he yawned, stretched himself out before the warm hearth, and slept.

127

In the morning the master and the mistress and the servants came back to the house.

"The ghost has gone," said the lad. "He is on his way to heaven. He won't come here again."

Then the master rejoiced and gave the lad a bag of gold. And the lad went merrily on his way.